On Strike Against God

Joanna Russ

The Crossing Press, Trumansburg, New York 14886

Library of Congress Cataloging in Publication Data

Russ,Joanna, 1937-
     On strike against God.

     Reprint. Originally published: Brooklyn, N.Y.:
Out & Out Books, 1980.
     I. Title.
PS3568.U76306   1985   813'.54   85-21320
ISBN 0-89594-186-4 (pbk.)

AUTHOR'S NOTE

My apologies to friends whose houses, dogs, gardens, mannerisms, clothing, and landscapes I have stolen for this book.

I have also stolen literary quotations. "Indefinable rapture" comes from Mary Ellmann's *Thinking About Women* (Harcourt Brace, Jovanovich, New York, 1968, p. 95). The various quotes from literary women are as follows: "How are we fallen! fallen by mistaken rules"—Anne, Countess of Winchilsea; "Women live like Bats or Owls, labour like Beasts, and die like Worms"—Margaret Cavendish, Duchess of Newcastle, both quoted by Virginia Woolf in *A Room of One's Own* (Harcourt, Brace, & World, New York, 1957, pp. 62 and 64). "Anyone may blame me who likes" is the beginning of the famous feminist outburst in Charlotte Bronte's *Jane Eyre*; "How good it must be to be a man when you want to travel," is quoted by Tillie Olsen from Rebecca Harding Davis's letter to a friend in Olsen's biographical essay on Davis in *Life in the Iron Mills* (The Feminist Press, Old Westbury, New York, 1972, p. 101). "John laughs at me but one expects that in marriage" occurs in Charlotte Perkins Gilman's *The Yellow Wallpaper* (The Feminist Press, Old Westbury, New York, 1973, p. 6). "It had all been a therapeutic lie. The mind was powerless to save her. Only a man—" is part of Mary McCarthy's story, "Ghostly Father, I Confess" in *The Company She Keeps* (Harcourt, Brace & World, New York, 1942, p. 302). The last quotation, "I/Revolve in my/Sheath of impossibles—" is part of the eleventh stanza of "Purdah" in Sylvia Plath's *Winter Trees* (Harper & Row, New York, 1972, p. 41).

Some of the above have undergone minor revisions, but there are no major ones.

For those interested, the strike referred to in the title is the shirtwaist-makers' strike of 1909-1910 which occurred in New York and Philadelphia. It was the first general strike of its kind and the first large strike of women workers in this country. It involved between ten and twenty thousand working women, most between the ages of sixteen and twenty-five. They held out for thirteen weeks in midwinter. One magistrate charged a striker: "You are on strike against God and Nature, whose prime law it is that man [sic] shall earn his bread in the sweat of his brow. You are on strike against God." Details may be found in Eleanor Flexner's *Century of Struggle* (Atheneum, New York, 1970, pp. 241-243).

"You are on strike against God"—said by a nineteenth-century American judge to a group of women workers from a textile mill. He was right, too, and I don't wonder at him. What I do wonder is where did they get the nerve to defy God? Because you'd think something would interfere with them, give them nervous headaches, hit them, muddle them, nag at them (at the very least) and prohibit them from daring to do it, just as something interferes with me, too, tries to keep me away from certain regions. As I write this the cold March rain is turning the new growth of the trees and bushes an intenser yellow and red, a sort of phantom fall in the tangle of weeds and bramble outside my window. But something doesn't want me to think about that. It's too beautiful. I once had a friend called Rose, whom I'd known for years, who lived in a slum that no matter how she painted the walls, it still looked rotten. The last time I ever saw her was just before I started teaching; I was twenty-nine. I went to visit her in East New York (Brooklyn) where she still lived with her mother and we talked, as we always did, about art and about the college professor she'd been in love with for years, a man much older than she. Rose and I went to high school together. It's this long-drawn-out business of interpreting his glances, his casual remarks, how he shakes her hand. She's got it all elaborately figured out. When I visited her she was putting away her three suits, her two scarves, her one sweater, her two changes of junk jewelry—all Rose has. She lays it out exquisitely in her bureau drawers and enjoys the sensation of living light. It's cheap but she takes endless time choosing it and laundering or cleaning it. (She works as an accountant, but not often, so she hasn't much money.) Whenever Rose decides to renounce the world she feels so good that she goes out to the movies and calls friends that very night. When I was there her mother had the TV on in the living room of that very little house—they live in a section of dilapidated clap-board houses, iron gates over all the storefronts at night, lots of weeds. Her mother's great pride was a pink, plastic table-cloth and matching plastic curtains in the living room, a vinyl-topped table for the TV. Rose had just repainted her own room with quick-drying paint; she was arranging her clothes, she who never goes out (hardly) and telling me in great detail about her fantastically complicated, draining, difficult, un-happy love affair with this man, which would be consum-mated (I suppose) in about twenty years when he was seventy and she almost fifty. She's very, very fat and good-looking, with a fat woman's strange and awesome smoothness, her monumental (and fake) physical serenity.

I said, "I'm in love, I'm in love again. Rose, did you hear me?"

She went on talking, folding and re-folding her clothes, turning toward me her witty, careful, pointed glance, so imita-tive of happiness. She knew I didn't mean it. At that time I didn't, and I don't know why I said it. Rose was preparing to leave the world again, which meant she would be very un-happy in a week or so. She didn't even listen to me. She was telling me how her mother had once seen her walking in front of a speeding car when she was a child and hadn't warned her.

I left her wallpapering her much-loved, much-tended little corner of hell.

Not really being in love then. Heavens, no. Not even think-ing about it. Without love there's nothing to bring into focus what's outside oneself, like (let us say) the soul of things non-human as manifested in the quiet clearness of a hillside in late winter, the place I live now, from the yellow grass-stems to the pebbles to the cut made for the road to pass through—all this in the misty graying-out of the Pennsylvania hills, the regular, rocking line of the ancient flood-plain, the occasional foun-tains of yellow-green where the willows are coming alive, red where it's some kind of bush, all these harmless, twiggy nerve-centers, the animate part of the great World Soul. Harmless until now, anyway. Landscape has a dangerous and deceiving repose, unlike cats or dogs who have eyes with which they can (gulp!) look right at you and sometimes do just that, as if they were persons, looking out of their own consciousness into yours and embarrassing and aweing you. Wild animals are only mobile bits of landscape. Until you learn better, you think that a landscaped world can't hurt you or please you, you needn't bother about its soul, you needn't be wary of its good looks.

Until you learn better.

I went out one night last August to look for my friend Jean, who's a graduate student in Classics here. The small town I work in (I teach English) has a collegiate appendix stuck on one end, two small streets on the hill down from the University, and in the more important block, the one restaurant that stays open throughout August, even after summer school has closed, the kind of place that's called Joe's, Charlie's, or Kent's; you know what I mean. Earlier in the evening there had been clouds sailing across the moon, up there in that deep inky-blue; so it was obvious to everyone that it was going to get much warmer or much colder by morning. I passed the melancholy parking meters (unused now), the pizza carry-out, the electronics parts store (closed), the laundry, the drugstore, the Indian boutique, the piano somebody has stuck on a sturdy pole and painted aluminum-color to advertise a private house that sells pianos—this looks very odd under the street lights and is really the damnedest thing I have ever seen. I'm going to look for Jean, the Twenty-Six Year Old Wonder: the eternal shield of her large sunglasses, her absurdly romantic long dresses (mauve or purple), her beautiful, square, pale, Swedish face, the tough muscles in her arms from three months on crutches (after a skiing accident in which she smashed her kneecap).

But she wasn't there. Nobody was, I mean nobody I know. There was someone I'd met at a faculty cocktail party, if you can call it met, but I ignored him because I really had thought that Jean would be there, or somebody. And I might have seen him in a play, not met him, I mean he might have been one of the Community Players; that's embarrassing. So I jumped when that fellow came over right after I'd sat down, I mean the unfriend, smiling suavely and saying, "Waiting for someone?" And what can you say when you jumped, when you thought you didn't know him, when you *don't* know him, not really? Are you going to turn down the chance? That's a lovely way to end up with no chances at all. And I'm thirty-eight. He frowned and said uneasily, "Um, can I sit down?" I'm not going to be mean. Four years ago—but it's different now— four years ago was my Israeli graduate student whom I picked up here out of sheer desperation right after I'd moved here (from another college five hundred miles away), sheer desperate loneliness (and because I knew I had to learn how to pick up men in bars)—he approved of my not wanting car doors opened for me like most demanding American women (but none of that pierced my ghastly haze of distress) and told me his views on America and the politics of campus revolution and what he was studying and why and what I should be studying and why. I said yes, yes, yes, oh yes, not even telling him I was a teacher, gibbering like anything out of sheer terror at existence (I had just got divorced, too) and later blew up at him when he tried to kiss me "because you're so understanding." Because it was a fake. Because he wasn't there. Because I wasn't there. Because he didn't know that I knew that he didn't know what I knew and didn't want to know.

Yes, dear, oh yes yes yes.

Why do men shred napkins? Three out of four napkin-shredders (rough estimate) are male. Female napkin-shredders are really napkin-strippers, i.e., they tear napkins into little strips, not shreds. But men who tear napkins tear them to shreds.

My new napkin-shredder sat down, a little dark fellow in Bermuda shorts and knee socks, and Goddamnit there went his hand out for the very first napkin. Blindly, appetitively seeking. Do you think I could ask him? Do you think I could say: Please, why are you tearing that there napkin into shred-type pieces? (Or pieces-type shreds, possibly.) Why? Why? Why? Oh, put your hands in your lap and leave the napkin alone!

Now, now, he's as nervous as you are, dear.

I said, "Your napkin—"

"What?" he said, alarmed.

I shook my head to indicate it was nothing. First we'll talk about the weather, that's number one, and then I'll listen appreciatively to his account of how hard it is to keep up a suburban home, that's number two, and then he'll complain about the number of students he's got, that's number three, and then he'll tell me something complimentary about my looks, that's number four, and then he'll finally get to talk about His Work.

"I've got an article coming out next May in the *Journal of the Criticism of Criticism*," he said.

"Oh, congratulations!" I said. "It's such a fine place. They don't keep you waiting, do they? Like *Parameter Studies*."

(My analyst and I often discussed—years ago—my compulsion to always have the last word with men. We worked on it for months but we never got anywhere.)

"They didn't keep *me* waiting," says Napkin Shredder (thus neatly dodging any mention by me of my seven articles in *Parameter*); "Perhaps you saw my articles there—the imagery of the nostril in Rilke?"

I made myself look frail and little. "Oh, no," I said. "I just can't keep up, you know."

(So far, so good.)

He then told me what his article in C of C was about and how he was going to make it into a book, none of which I particularly wanted to hear—nor did I want to talk about mine, which I also find extremely boring, why inflict it on strangers?—but it's a sign they like you, so I listened attentively, from time to time saying "Mm" and "Mm hm" and watching the front window of the restaurant in the hope that Jean might walk by. *Why are you telling me all this?*—but that's a line for the movies. Besides I know why. And, as usual, the burden of maturity, compassion, consideration, understanding, tolerance, etc. etc. is on me. Again.

"Oh my, really?" I said. (I don't know at what.) He beamed. He began to tell me about a grant he was going to get. He told me this in a confidential way (leaning very close across the table) and I thought in a confused fashion—or my manners must have been slipping—or I'd been watching the front window too long—anyway, one ought to help, oughtn't one?—so I answered without thinking (my analyst and I worked on this too but we didn't get anywhere):

"Don't do it. Just don't do it. They make you work too hard

for your money. I know; I've gotten grants from them twice."

There was a strained silence. Perhaps I'd discouraged him. He told me the names of his last four articles, which had been published in various places; he told me where, and then he told me what the editors had said about them (the articles). He was talking with that edge in his voice that means I've provoked something or done something impolite or failed to do something I should've done; you are supposed to show an intelligent interest, aren't you? You're supposed to encourage. So I analyzed the strengths of all those separate editors and journals and praised all of them; I said I admired him and it was really something to get into those journals, as I very well knew.

"I often wonder why women have careers," said Shredded Napkin suddenly, showing his teeth. I don't think he can possibly be saying what I think he's saying. He isn't, of course. Never mind. I'll stand this because Reality is dishing it out and I suppose I ought to learn to adjust to it. Besides, he may be sincere. There is a human being in there. At least he isn't telling me about something he read in the paper on women's liberation and then laughing at it.

"Oh goodness, I don't know, the same thing that makes a man decide, I suppose," I said, trying to look bland and disarming. "Cheers."

"Cheers," he said. The drinks had come. He opened his mouth to say something and then appeared to relent; he traced circles with his forefinger on the table. Then he said, leaning forward:

"You're strange animals, you women intellectuals. Tell me: what's it like to be a woman?"

I took my rifle from behind my chair and shot him dead. "It's like that," I said. No, of course I didn't. Shredder is only trying to be nice; he would really like me best with a fever of 102 and laryngitis, but then he's not like everybody, is he? Or does he say what they only think? It's not worth it, hating, and I am going to be mature and realistic and not care, not care. Not any more.

"At least you're still—uh—decorative!" he said, winking.

Don't care. Don't care.

I said quickly, "Oh my, I've got to go," and he looked disappointed. He's beginning to like me. I am a better and better audience as I get numbed, and although I've played this game of Impress You before (and won it, too—though I don't like either of the prizes; winning is too much like losing) I'm too tired to go on playing tonight. Will he insist on taking me home? Will he ask me out? Will he fight over the bill? Will he start making remarks about women being this or that, or tell me I'm a good woman because I'm not competitive?

Oh why is it such awful work?

Shredder (coloring like a schoolboy) says he hopes I won't laugh but he has a few—uh—odd hobbies besides his work; he's always been tremendously interested in science, you know (he tosses off a frivolous reference to C. P. Snow and the "two cultures") and would I (he says, shyly) like to hear a lecture next Thursday on the isomeric structure of polylaminates? As I would, actually, but not with him. (His ears turned pink and he looked suddenly rather nice. But will it last?) I don't want to make a bafflefield—sorry, battlefield—of my private life. Bafflefiend! Goodbye, Mr. Bafflefiend. I will leave Shredder and go look for a Good, Gentle-but-Firm, Understanding, Virile Man. That's what my psychoanalyst used to keep telling me to do. To avoid quarreling I let Shredder pay for the drinks (a bargain for him but not for me); to avoid endless squabbling insistencies I let him walk me around the corner to what I said was my home; and to duck the usual unpleasant scene ("What's the matter with you? Don't you like men?") gave him my—entirely fictitious—telephone number. I waited inside the building until he'd vanished uphill and then slipped out into the street and started off in the opposite direction. Spoiled, spoiled. All spoiled. My psychoanalyst (who has in reality been dead for a decade) came out of the clouds and swooped at me as I trudged home, great claws at the ready, batwings black against the moon, dripping phosphorescent slime. Etcetera. (All the way from New York.)

You will never get married!

All right, all right, Count Draculule.

You fear fulfillment.

Buzz off, knot-head.

Your attitude toward your femininity is ambivalent. You hope and yet you fear. You attract men, but you drive them away. What a tangle is here!

I giggled.

You do not like men, Esther. You have penis envy.

They have humanity envy. They don't like me.

Come now, men are attracted to you, aren't they?

That's not what I said, kiddo.

He comes back every once in a while, very stern and severe; then he goes back up into a cloud to clean his fangs. We get along. After a while you tame your interior monsters, it's only natural. I don't mean that it ever stops; but it stops mattering. I trudged down the hill and up the hill to home (then up the stairs). My kitchen is always a greeting; I don't know why. I don't like to cook. Yet my apartment always strikes me—after each small absence—as something I've created myself, with my own two hands, something solid and colorful and nice, like an analogue of myself. It greets me. You can see that this is going to require an awful lot of (naturalistic) padding while I walk home, climb steps, sleep, or go from one room to another. But in recompense I will tell you what I was thinking all the way home in that chilly, fragrant, August night: I was thinking that I felt sexually dead, that I was perpetually tired, that my body was cold and self-contained, that I had been so for eleven years, ever since my divorce, and that nothing I had done or could do or would ever be able to do would ever bring me back to life. I didn't like that. Not that it was a tragic feeling; it was only something mildly astonishing (in the middle of all the things I do like and enjoy). It amazed me. As I threw the windows open to the night I thought that at least I had fed my showy, neurotic, insecure, exhibitionistic personality to the full over the last few years, that in this one way (and many others) I was very happy, I enjoyed myself tremendously, but there was something else I didn't have, another way in which I was deprived. Yet a mild feeling, believe me. At least so far.

I'll tell you something: my psychoanalyst (I mean the real one) used to ride around Manhattan on a motorcycle. It was his one eccentricity. I think he was secretly proud of it. Whenever patients in our group (what a word, *patients*) got audibly worried about this rather dangerous habit, he would (I think) be secretly delighted; he would beam without apparently being aware of how pleased he was, and then this tall, balding businessman would say, "O let us analyze your anxiety." He never analyzed his own liking for the motorcycle. He was thrown from it in a collision with an automobile and died in the street, leaving behind a widow (badly provided for) and two small children. He was younger than I am now. You may gather that I didn't entirely like the man and that's true—but when he comes zooping down from his black cloud, fangs a-quiver, I think of his death and it warms me. It pleases me. The man was such a fool. I try to make myself sorry by thinking of his wife and children—there's his poor wife, compelled to believe all that nonsense, yes, and live it too (don't tell me she never sneaked a peek in Freud, just to see). Did she have the wrong kind of orgasm? Did she succeed in renouncing her masculine protest? Hypocritically I try to make myself cry, thinking that I should feel sorry for anyone in such an accident, all that blood over the street, etc., the twisted motorcycle, etc. Then I'm not pleased. Then I have a very different reaction.

Snoork! I laugh.

To be sexually dead....

Well, people pretend to be better than they are. That used to mean frigid, but now it means something else. The truth that's never told today about sex is that you aren't good at it, that you don't like it, that you haven't got much. That you're at sea and unhappy. When I was married I never lay back and opened my knees without feeling (with a sinking of the heart, an inexpressible anguish) "Here we go again," a phrase I couldn't explain to my analyst and can't now. I think it was because my thighs hurt. I did get some mild pleasure out of the whole business, I don't want to misrepresent that, but not much; I could never get my feet down on the bed when I put my knees up (my tendons were too tight) so after a few minutes my knees and thighs would begin to hurt; then they'd hurt a lot and if I turned over and we did it the other way my face would get pushed into the mattress and I didn't like that. I couldn't move at all that way. And if I sat on top it was lonely and I couldn't relax and I knew I was supposed to relax (all the books said it) because if I pushed or tried to take control, then I wouldn't come. But my husband never seemed to know what to do. *To be made love to*—that was the point. Only I was no good at it.

What I cannot convey is the intense confusion I felt when I tried even to think about it.

Cures: my analyst told me not to try for orgasm at all, so I knew I was wrong to be hung up about it because it wasn't important; or rather it was so important that you had to treat it as if it wasn't important (or you would never have it); so for a long time I could never think of myself sexually at all without intense confusion (as I've said) and great personal pain.

Have masochistic fantasies—but that's much too close to real life.

Pretend you're a man—I did that when I was fourteen. But that's forbidden (and impossible). I used to daydream (twenty-four years ago, can you believe it was so long? I can't) that I was a man making love with another man. Which still strikes me as fairly bizarre, if you start thinking about the transformations of identity involved. I told my analyst.

He: In this—ah—daydream, are you the active or the passive partner?

Me: What?

He: (patiently) Psychology knows that in homosexual pairs, one man is always the active partner in love-making and the other man is always passive. Now which do you imagine yourself being?

But here an abyss opened beneath my feet. I still am not really sure why. The truth is that I felt the coming battle without being able to name a thing about it; was it that I wanted to say one thing and would be made to say another? Or ought to say another? Or must say one thing and must not say it at the same time? I didn't know. I knew one thing only and that was crystal-clear: *I was going to lose.* So it was with the

simultaneous sense of sneaking home safe and yet being intolerably—oh, just intolerably! coerced—that I replied very
haltingly:

Me: (blush) Um...passive. The passive one.

He: (delighted) Ah! So you really are the woman, you see.
Which is not so. It's just not so.

"You know," said my analyst, "there's no reason you can't
tell your husband what you'd like him to do to you. Women
ought to be aggressive in bed."

Me: Lost again. I always lose. (But I didn't say it. I smiled a
sick, feeble, little smile and agreed.)

What else could I do?

I remembered summer camp at the age of twelve when I
necked with my best friend (we all did) but wouldn't touch her
breasts because I was too embarrassed. The next summer
everyone had apparently forgotten what we had done the
summer before. (A point of peculiar integration from which
everything has gone most definitely down-hill.)

I desired my husband—but it didn't work. I experience the
same muddle-headedness when I try to remember *what* didn't
work. I have no words for it.

Having a heart-felt crush on beautiful, gentle, helpless,
intelligent Danny Kaye at age twelve and a half. I seem to be
going through the right phases at the right times. Still, I keep
wanting to rescue him from things. Can that be right? (Is it
sadism?)

The best solution (and the one I pursued after my divorce):
Not to think about it at all.

Jean dropped over for breakfast the next morning, which
was Sunday, bringing with her black cherry ice cream and
bacon, both of which we ate. This is an honor; she seldom
spends money for luxuries because she lives on a fellowship in
a co-op dowtown. Sat around the kitchen, loath to leave (the
most crucial room in the house), drinking endless cups of tea
until the memory of the black cherry ice cream became un-
pleasantly dim. There was a wonderful surfeit of odds and
ends on the table. I had been trying to plan the day's affairs to
avoid the premise that I had absolutely nothing left to do, for
a three-months' vacation (my vacation, an academic one) is

like the jungles in H. Rider Haggard: first your little traveling
party goes through the harmless fringes of the first few days,
everything looking only mildly sinister; then there's the thick-
ening growth and the awful feeling that it'll never end, and
then you start losing people—beating the bushes for them,
holloa-ing for them (but it's no use)—and finally all those
early glimpses of prehistoric monsters and strange footprints
(or arrows or axe-heads buried in tree-trunks) pay off, so to
speak; I mean that your camp is attacked in the brief tropical
dawn by Beast Men or a Phagocytus Giganticus who eats the
native guide, the heroine's father (a scientist), his assistant,
and all the maps, leaving our heroine alone in the jungle she
now knows contains almost two months more of vacation and
nothing whatever to do. There I was. With the hope that I
could eventually walk in a sort of trance to the foot-hills (I
mean that you will get used to it) and begin to climb. But my
apartment's been burnished to a high gloss (including cutting
fuzz off the rug with a nail scissor, honest) and I've also
decided not to move to another apartment. The dinosaur's
eaten the map.

I told all this to Jean.

"Look!" she said, and she drew three interlocking circles on
her napkin (like the beer ad).

"Mimetic," she said. "Didactic. Romantic." And went off
into something I couldn't follow.

"This morning I dreamed I saw Death at the foot of my
bed," she said. "He was reading a newspaper. Hiding his face
in it. Banal, really."

"Work is a real blessing," she said. (She's right.)

I stirred my tea. I played with my food. Brightening up, she
told me how the cooperative's dog had caught a rattlesnake,
courageously biting it in two although it made him vomit. So-
and-so had made noodle pudding. So-and-so was trying to fix
the phonograph. It's a loose practical association, nothing
very striking; I mean you must not think of it as any close,
mystical, hippie-dippy sort of thing because it's not. Jean
studies mathematics for fun, makes her own clothes as a
recreation, can do anything, is ferociously private. Stupid
Philpotts (the cooperative's dog) is a cross between an Afghan

and an English sheepdog; first he chases the sheep, then he knits them into sweaters. I couldn't stop laughing. Jean, whose arrogance toward other people is often terrifying, was staring dreamily ahead, one hand curled in her lap. Stupid Philpotts (she told me) is large and skinny and covered with immense amounts of curly white hair (which quite conceals his face); if you lift the hair, you see his beautiful, intelligent, long-lashed eyes, which gleam at you like lovely jewels. He was missing for eight days last winter and came back with ice-balls the size of golf-balls frozen into his hair. And diarrhea from eating garbage.

"Those damned bastards," said my friend, thinking of something else entirely.

In the summer, in my apartment, you can always go into the living room and look over the hills. Actually you can do it in winter, too, because the setting sun—in the course of one year—describes an arc that stretches from the Southernmost window of the living room (in December) to the Northernmost end of the study window (in June). You can watch the sunset every day of the year through my enormous windows. Overhead the third-floor tenants were walking about, a nuisance that somewhat dilutes the pleasure I take in my windows. Jean had sat here exactly eight months ago, basting the lining of a coat; she often hauls her sewing around with her. But don't think of this as anything domestic or feminine in the ordinary sense; Jean's sewing is part of her perfectionism. It's armor plate.

"Those—!" she said again. Some teacher of hers (she told me) making passes at her in spite of her saying no; some teacher's wife (at another time) badmouthing women graduate students with that venomous sweetness that shows you how very "feminine" the woman is—she can't get angry openly, not even at another woman. Pathetic and awful, both of them. And the men in the collective not wanting to do certain kinds of work.

"Men run the world," said Jean. "Men are people; therefore people run the world."

"Evil people," I said. "Are you a man-hater?"

"Don't be silly" (absent-mindedly).

Am I a man-hater? Man-haters are evil, sick freaks who ought to be locked up and treated until they change their ideas. If you think (under those conditions) that I'm going to admit *anything,* you're nuts. Let's just say that I don't like to sit still and smile a lot. And I would rather not hate anyone (virtuous me!); that is, I would rather there was no reason for it.

"Jean," I said, "did I ever tell you about my friend Shirley?" (Shirl the Girl who went into an expensive private mental hospital in New York and came out insisting *she had to wear stockings* or they'd get her again. "You gotta conform," she'd said to me grimly.)

"Yes. Many times."

"Oh," I said, shaping the O sound very purely (but silently) with my lips. Playing. Bored.

"I would rather not hate anyone," said Jean, pausing in her work (she had brought a pair of white gabardine slacks with her, to hem by hand). The Duchess Look: objective, dispassionate, not pleased. I told you that last night was very clear, active, and cold; now huge black clouds are rising on the Southwestern horizon, the place our weather comes from through a pass in the hills. Leaves, twigs, and bits of detritus are being blown all over the place. The light's turning green. I went about shutting windows and wondering if the rain-gutter would fall into the garden again—not that we have a real garden, I'm talking about the rather elementary piece of lawn the landlady pays the boy next door to mow once in a while and our two unkempt forsythia bushes. The house is old, and besides providing a sounding-board for footsteps, it has trouble with some of its trim. Jean and I sat and watched the faraway part of the town (in the valley) disappear under rain; there was a *crack!* and you could see the streets darkening one by one. Sound of machine-gun fire or round-shot in buckets. Myriads of dashes on the screens first, then on the windowpanes. Pockmarks on the porch roof. Then with another rattling slam the windows became invisible and the whole house ran with water, a real summer storm. The air in the living room was already getting stuffy. Stupid Philpotts (said Jean) would be hiding under somebody's bed now, although what all this meant to him, deep in his doggy mind, nobody could tell.

"Ah! *he* knows," said I. Jean giggled. She fiddled with my radio and then turned it off. Our storm withdrew down the valley and along the lake, grumbling and muttering. Eight minutes after it had begun we opened the windows; the temperature had dropped fifteen degrees during the rain, but the sun was coming out, straight overhead and very hot. It was noon. No, it was high noon, sun-time. I don't know if a clearing storm can ever be followed by a rise in temperature unless it's hot beforehand, but that's what happened. Summer was back again. Proper August: humid air and puddles. I looked at Jean again, wanting to say something-or-other and expecting she'd be back at her work, but she was looking past me, the Duchess look gone from her face, all the cynicism gone, the laziness, the bitterness. Through my bedroom window, where the sun rises in December, through the Southeastern window just opposite the direction of the departing storm, was a double rainbow which the Australians call mother and daughter. So rare, so lovely. Everything a vivid emerald green in which the mailbox on the corner shone like 1940's lipstick. Those strange, aniline hues you never see anywhere in nature, and at the earthly end (guaranteed or your money back) King Solomon's Mines. (I'm in the foothills at last.) It's not possible to stay unhappy. I took Jean's hand and we waltzed clumsily around the room. We said, "Isn't it lovely?" as people do, but we really meant more than we could say: this double rainbow, a completely circular ice-bow on Cape Cod, a seagull against the sun, cherry trees in the Brooklyn Botanical Gardens, being wheeled there when I was a child, times like these.

We meant: It's a sign.

Even if it were permissible to hate men, I don't think I would. You can hate some of the men all of the time and you can hate all of the men some of the time. Tell the truth or bust! (We shall not bust.) I remember walking down the city streets years ago and being suddenly amazed into a stab of love and admiration for my beautiful, gentle husband with whom (as I told you) I could not make love. Why did we ever separate? Something must have shown on my face, for people stared. I remember being endlessly sick to death of this world which isn't mine and won't be for at least a hundred years; you'd be surprised how I can go through almost a whole day thinking I live here and then some ad or something comes along and gives me a nudge—just reminding me that not only do I not have a right to be here; I don't even exist. Since I crawled into this particular ivory tower it has not been better, hearing about the typical new man in the department and his work and his pay and his schedule and his wife and his children (me? my department), well that's only comedy, but what goes right to my heart is the endless smiling of the secretaries where I work, the endless anxiety to please. The anxiety. Like my husband, coming home on the bus with me from my shrink and blurting out, "There's only you and me, what does he mean, *the* marriage!"

Still, sex was no good with him. Seeing a double rainbow with Jean and waltzing around the room (clumsily but solemnly) has somehow enabled me to remember that sex with my husband was in fact very bad, the badness of it being (as I remember) a good measure of the truly vast number of things I could not—then—manage to remember. Or rather, I labored so conscientiously to remember to forget them; if only I'd had a worse memory! But I didn't. I am a good, earless, eyeless girl who walks past construction workers without hearing or seeing anything and the last time I hung upside-down by my knees from the top of the jungle gym I was five years old. I wonder what I made of that upside-down world. Already dainty and good, not liking to have smudges on my dress (when I remembered) and setting my dolls to school like my elementary-school teacher aunt, dressing them in appropriate costumes for the season (which practice I continue with myself, by the way), and spending a lot of time fussing over which of them was the tallest and which the shortest because they had to be put in a row of graduated height for school. I wrapped up my best doll and took her downstairs once to see a hailstorm. But I got dirty, too. And I liked the world upside-down (having bat blood) and longed fiercely to get up in the clouds, which you could only do if they were "down"—i.e. hanging on the jungle gym. I would swing my way absent-mindedly to the top like a monkey and then hang there, stern and sensible, full of cosmic awe. There's a picture of this dead little five-year-old woman looking at the inside of her first post office, rows and rows of post-office boxes right up to the ceiling; she's hanging on to the knobs of two of them with an indecipherable—perhaps stunned—expression. I'm looking at a jail. The Rose-Growers' Association gardens where we went every week-end was my mother; my father was the post office (because he worked in an office); I myself was the stone lion outside the post office. There's a picture of me sitting astride it, looking uncomfortable and exalted. In the earliest family snapshot of all (I mean after the wet-lump stage, which does not show personality, at least in a kodak) I am peeking dramatically around the corner of a city fire hydrant, my face smeared beautifully all over with chocolate ice cream. It all looks so good: don't give a damn about anybody and having a good time. I am told that these short people are still alive somewhere, possibly inside the great, grand palimpsest of Me, and somewhere at the center (like a kernel in a nut) the archaic idol, all red wrinkles, who got wrapped screaming in a blanket (covering her enlarged vulva—this is true, you know, for a few days after birth) who sucked in foodstuff at one end and squirted product-stuff out the other, like a sea-anemone. But this I don't believe. You're supposed to break your teeth on this archaic center if you bite too deeply into things—but I find the howler monkey, the wanter, the hater, the screamer, far too modern and present to think of her as the leftovers from a baby. And who could call a wet lump *she?* You might as well call it Irving. What has truly never left me is the post office boxes (which I rather liked; they certainly looked powerful and important) and the jungle gym. Witches do everything upside-down and backwards; they go in where they should go out, and out when they should go in. Or flat. Like all women. So get used to seeing everything upside-down as you read this.

But the name is bad. The name is awful. I mean that

everyone I've met, everyone I know well (unless they're lying, as I always am in a social situation—you don't think I want to get locked up, do you?)—anyway, every female friend of mine seems to have accepted in some sense that she is a woman, has decided All right, I am a woman; rolls that name "woman" over and over on her tongue, trying to figure out what it means, looks at herself in a full-length mirror, trying to understand, "Is that what they mean by Woman?" They're ladies. They're pretty. They're quiet and cheerful. They want a better deal, maybe, but they're easy-going, they have a certain serenity, they're *women*. Perhaps they've lost something, perhaps they've hidden something. When they were sixteen they could say, "I'm a *girl*, aren't I?" and not be stupefied, stunned, confused, and utterly defeated by the irrelevant idiocy of the whole proceeding.

I'm not a woman. Never, never. Never was, never will be. I'm a something-else. My breasts are a something-else's breasts. My (really rather spiffy) behind is a something-else's behind. My something-else's face with its prophetic thin bones, its big sunken eyes, my long long-bones, my stretched-out hands and feet, my hunched-over posture, all belong to a something-else. I have a something-else's uterus, and a clitoris (which is not a woman's because nobody ever mentioned it while I was growing up) and something-else's straight, short hair, and every twenty-five days blood comes out of my something-else's vagina, which is a something-else doing its bodily housekeeping. This something-else has wormed its way into a university teaching job by a series of impersonations which never ceases to amaze me; for example, it wears stockings. It smiles pleasantly when it's called an honorary male. It hums a tune when it's told that it thinks like a man. If I ever deliver from between my smooth, slightly marbled something-else thighs a daughter, that daughter will be a something-else until unspeakable people (like my parents—or yours) get hold of it. I might even do bad things to it myself, for which I hope I will weep blood and be reincarnated as a house plant. I do not want a better deal. I do not want to make a deal at all. *I want it all.* They got to my mother and made her a woman, but they won't get me.

Something-elses of the world, unite!
Do you think Jean is—might be—a something-else?

Sally, Louise, Jean, and I were watching a bad movie on TV.
Behold a handsome, virile, football-player actor pretending
to be an eminent scientist. It was one of those movies in which
a computer takes over the world and you jolly well wish it
would—anything's better than the people. I notice that the
Amurricans are all glamorous mesomorphs under thirty-five
but the Rooshians are fat and middle-aged. So I'm in trouble
with art, too. Sally and Louise are visiting—old acquaintances
of Jean's, not really friends, for they're much older than she is
(she's twenty-six)—with a dog named Lady who barely got
into the apartment before she zipped frantically under the
sofa and stayed there for the entire visit, at the end of which
she came out very stiff and stretching herself as if she'd had
rheumatism. Lady's afraid of new places. Lady, I was told, is a
Belgian sheepdog with a tendency to herd strange children—
that's funny to tell about if nobody takes you to court over it;
nor is it funny or pleasant for the children who have their
heels nipped, I imagine.
What are Sally and Louise like?
Well, they look like—well, like anybody. They aren't glamorous. From a distance they look young (that's the blue jeans);
but they're grown women in their late thirties, even as you and
I; Jean knew them when they were English teachers here. I
don't know them. Louise is the chunky one who wears huge,
fashion-model sunglasses and tried very patiently to coax
Lady out from under my sofa (Lady growled and retreated).
Sally is the skinny one and talks a lot. If she weren't so friendly
and civilized, one feels, she'd be into your refrigerator instantly, or examining your drapes for blister rust or your
cupboards for teacup blight. Not that she's pushy; she's just
interested. Truth to tell, Louise is not so plump nor is Sally so
skinny; it's only that there's little to say about women who
don't project themselves dramatically by way of makeup or
dress. And there was the weariness of their eight-hour drive
from Virginia. In both ways totally unlike my friend Jean, who

was being very WASP college-girl fresh and beautiful: her hair caught back by a green ribbon, her bell-bottomed green pants, a man's white shirt tied together in front. All of us, I think, had the academic drabness in which everything has run to voice, so I remember Sally's quick, brilliant, insistent hammer-blows (the voice of a short woman who's on her way to becoming a time-bomb because nobody ever takes her seriously) and from time to time Louise's slow, deeper, ironic, Southern interruptions, one hand going down to rub the dog's nose. Lady didn't say a word. And Jean is always just Jean.

What did we talk about?

I don't remember. We talked so hard and sat so still that I got cramps in my knees. We had too many cups of tea and then didn't want to leave the table to go to the bathroom because we didn't want to stop talking. You will think we talked of revolution but we didn't. Nor did we talk of our own souls. Nor of sewing. Nor of babies. Nor of departmental intrigue. It was politics if by politics you mean the laboratory talk that characters in bad movies are perpetually trying to convey (unsuccessfully) when they Wrinkle Their Wee Brows and say (valiantly—dutifully—after all, *they* didn't write it) "But, Doctor, doesn't that violate Finagle's Constant?" I staggered to the bathroom, released floods of tea, and returned to the kitcken to talk. It was professional talk. It left me grey-faced and with such concentration that I began to develop a headache. We talked about Mary Ann Evans' loss of faith, about Emily Brontë's isolation, about Charlotte Brontë's blinding cloud, about the split in Virginia Woolf's head and the split in her economic situation. We talked about Lady Murasaki, who wrote in a form that no respectable man would touch, Hroswit, a little name whose plays "may perhaps amuse myself," Miss Austen, who had no more expression in society than a firescreen or a poker. They did not all write letters, write memoirs, or go on the stage. Sappho—only an ambiguous, somewhat disagreeable name. Corinna? The teacher of Pindar. Olive Schreiner, growing up on the veldt, wrote one book, married happily, and never wrote another. Kate Chopin wrote a scandalous book and never wrote another.

(Jean has written nothing.) There was M-ry Sh-ll-y who wrote you know what and Ch-rl-tt- P-rk-ns G-lm-n, who wrote one superb horror story and lots of sludge (was it sludge?), and Ph-ll-s Wh--tl-y who was black and wrote eighteenth century odes (but it was the eighteenth century) and Mrs. -nn R-dcl-ff- who wrote silly novels and M-rg-r-t C-v-nd-sh and Mrs. -d-n S--thw-rth and Mrs. G--rg-- Sh-ld-n and (Miss?) G--rg-tt- H-y-r and B-rb-r- C-rtl-nd and the legion of those, who writing, write not, like the dead Miss B--l-y of the poem who was seduced into bad practices (fudging her endings) and hanged herself in her garter. The sun was going down. I was blind and stiff. It's at this point that the computer (which has run amok and eaten Los Angeles) is defeated by some scientifically transcendent version of pulling out the plug; the furniture stood round us unknowing (though we had just pulled out the plug) and Lady, who got restless when people talked at such length because she couldn't understand it, stuck her head out from under the couch, looking for things to herd. We had talked for six hours, from one in the afternoon until seven; I had at that moment an impression of our act of creation so strong, so sharp, so extraordinarily vivid, that I could not believe all our talking hadn't led to something more tangible—mightn't you expect (at least) a little blue pyramid sitting in the middle of the floor? But there wasn't anything. I had a terrible shock, something so profound that I couldn't even tell what it was; for nothing had changed—the sun sank, the light breeze blew through my enormous open windows. The view over the hills was as splendid as ever. I looked for the cause in Lady, who had eased herself stiffly out from under the sofa with a plaintive whine of discomfort, I looked at the lamps, the tables, my floor-to-ceiling bookcase, my white walls, my blue rug and red curtains, my black-framed pictures of roses and robots. But nothing has exploded, or changed color, or turned upside down, or is speaking in verse. Nor had the wall opened to reveal a world-wide, three-dimensional, true-view television set playing for the enlightenment of the human race and our especial enjoyment, a correct, truly scientific (this time) film about a runaway computer in Los Angeles in which all the important roles were played by grey-haired, middle-aged women. That would violate everything. (The other way only we are violated.) Perhaps in the days of the Great Goddess (before everything went wrong) creation was both voluntary and involuntary, in the mind and in the body, so to bear the stars and planets—indeed, the whole universe—She had not only to grunt and sweat with the contractions of Her mind, but think profoundly, rationally, and heavily with Her womb.

Then the spontaneous remission. The healing. The Goddess's kindly and impatient gift. I started thinking again and the first thought was very embarrassing: I realized I had been staring very rudely at Jean, who was sitting in front of the window and whose breasts were silhouetted through her blouse by the late afternoon sun. I tried to tell all this to the others, but I think they were only amused. "We're brilliant," I said. "We're the great ones." (I meant: what those others say about us isn't true.)

"Sure," said Louise.

I wanted to say to Jean, I'm embarrassed because I saw the outline of your breasts and you're running around without a bra. But my head hurt.

"I'm dying of hunger," said Sally. "Let's go out."

(You see, we're the real people. We're the best. I don't mean that we're "as good as men" or that "everyone is equal" or that "people should be judged as individuals." I'm not referring to those others out there at all. It's a question of what's put at the center. See Copernicus and Galileo. I know you know all this, but indulge me. Listen to me. The roof has just come off the world and here is the Sun, who took Her broad, matron's face down behind the last, the Westernmost hill, and here is baby Night, who's leaning Her elbows on the cool sill of the East. She carries a fishing rod so that She can dangle the bright bob of setting Venus over the brow of the Sun. Something has vanished from the top of the sky, some lid or lens or fishbowl that's been closed oppressively over my head as long as I can remember and nobody ever even remarked upon it or criticized it or took the trouble to suggest that it might not be a good thing, that it might even be better if it were removed. I trailed after Jean to the door, thinking that I was making some other decision, too, but something I didn't understand, and that it was unsettling to feel voluntary action taking place in a region you can't even reach. Anyway, it's just one of my fantasies. And it doesn't matter. Not that it's something in me; it's only something strange in the way the world is put together, something about the way foundations of the world are arranged.

(But what is "it?"
(I don't know.)

My fantasies. Oh lord, my fantasies. The human bat fantasy about mating in mid-air. The Super-Woman fantasy (before the comic book). The hermit fantasy. The Theda Bara fantasy. The disguised lady as reckless hero fantasy (Zorra). I have a million of 'em. One of us who is writing this (we're a committee) was told by her mother that she was named Joan after Juana la Loca or Crazy Joanna, a poor Spanish Queen bereft of her wits who followed her husband's embalmed corpse around An-da-lu-*thee*-ya etc. for eighteen years. It's in the encyclopedia. Now this is a hell of a thing to put on your daughter. I found out last week that her real namesake was in fact the spiritual leader of the entire Western World and somebody who scared everyone so much they had to rearrange the succession of Popes (with two years left unaccounted for and one Pope John), efface her from the history books for four hundred years, and demand a physical examination of every candidate for the Papacy thereafter, lest they again get stuck with a woman (Brand X). I mean, of course, Pope Joan—or John VIII, Joannes in Latin. Not to mention the saint who came after her, which makes this particular name very powerful indeed.*

That poor mother was deceived. She had become abject.

It is very important, Boadicea, Tomyris, Cartismandua, Artemisia, Corinna, Eva, Mrs. Georgie Sheldon, *to find out for whom you were named.*

Queen Esther, my namesake, got down on her knees to save

---

*d. 855, anathematized *1601*. Oops.

her people, which is no great shakes, but Ruth—whose name means Compassion—said Whither thou goest, I will go too. *To her mother-in-law.*

Big news for all the Esthers and Stellas in the audience— your name means "star." Forget Hollywood. Stars, like women, are mythologized out of all reality. For example, the temperature at the core of Y Cygni, a young blue-violet star of impeccable background (the main sequence), is thirty-two million degrees Centigrade. This is also Epsilon Aurigae, that big, cool, unwieldy red giant, whose average temperature is a bare seven hundred degrees C but whose outer edges are as big around as the orbit of Uranus. And the neutron stars, denser than white dwarfs (20,000 times the density of water) and those even more collapsed but poetical persons who are supposed to disappear entirely from the known universe, at least to the eye (their immense gravitational fields trap the light trying to escape from their surfaces) but who remain at the center of an unexplained attraction—the disturbing center at a lot of nothing, you might say. Sylvia did this once or twice. If you're really ambitious, you might try to be a nova, which (says George Gamow in *The Life and Death of the Sun*, Mentor, 1959):

> *will blast into an intensity surpassing that of its normal state by a factor of several hundreds of thousands and, in some cases, even of several billions.*

(p. 155)

Or

> *an essentially different class of stellar explosions* [with a] *maximum luminosity on the average 10,000 times greater than that of ordinary novae and exceeding by a factor of several billions the luminosity of our Sun.*

(p. 157)

This part of the book is full of italics; I think even the author got scared. Moreover, a supernova is visible from Earth every three centuries and we're about due for one. Just think: *You might be it.*

Did you hear that, Marilyn? Did you hear that, Natalie,

Darlene, Shirley, Cheryl, Barbara, Dorine, Lori, Hollis, Debbi? Did you hear that, starlets? You needn't kneel to Ahasuerus. You needn't be a burnt offering like poor Joan. Practice the Phoenix Reaction and rise perpetually from your own ashes!—even as does our own quiet little Sun, cozy hearthlet that it is, mellow and mild as a cheese, with its external temperature of 6000 degrees Centigrade (just enough to warm your hands at) and its perhaps rather dismaying interior, whose temperature may range anywhere— in degrees Centigrade—from fifteen to twenty-one million. The sun's in its teens, fifteen to twenty-one. The really attractive years. The pretty period.

And that, says *my* bible, is what they mean by my name. That's an Esther. That's me.

Jean and I went to a party. It was given by Jean's parents, with Jean acting as a social slavey along with her younger sister, her younger brother being exempt and her older sister having married a tree manufacturer in Oregon—sorry, a lumber manufacturer. (Only God can make a tree and She seldom tries, nowadays.) It was mostly academic people, friends of Jean's parents, who are both biologists at the university agricultural and veterinary school, her father a full professor, well-paid, her mother a part-time researcher, unpaid. (Their work is far too esoteric for me to understand, let alone explain.) The first thing that happened at this party was that someone started a contest between the men and the women—there was one way in which women were physically superior to men, which involved standing two feet from a wall, putting your forehead against it, and then trying to raise a chair. It was something to do with leverage. Whatever the damned thing was, I wouldn't do it. They coaxed me but I wouldn't. "Aren't you interested in the differences between men and women?" they said. I said I thought we ought to judge people as individuals. What I really wanted to say was that if we were having a contest of physical abilities, I'd like to see some of the men give birth, but if you do that (I mean say it, not do it) you spend the rest of the evening fending off some extremely respectable character (sometimes, but not always, from the Middle East) who has been looking all his life for a free, independent woman to Talk Dirty With. Jean's parents had made her put on stockings so she was scratching herself as ungracefully as possible whenever anyone looked at her. She was sulky. The talk next turned to push-ups, which the men got very excited about (but I can't do push-ups either) and then to the more usual things, like weather, so it appeared that we might be getting out of the woods, but then somebody leaned across the coffee table (dropping ashes on the family's expensive but sturdy-and-practical rug—why is it that the only aesthetic people in science are the physicists?) and re-marked, looking rather pointedly at me:

"I hear someone's giving a paper on menstruation at the next MLA." The MLA is the Modern Language Association, a sort of English-teacher monopoly.

O giggle giggle giggle (all over the room).

Probably a eunuch, said I. Aloud I said:

"Come on, you're just making that up to tease me."

"Oh, no," he said. "Honestly. I wondered what you thought about it."

"Be serious," said I, brightly.

"But I am!" And he writhed a little, like Uriah Heep. "I want to know your opinion of it."

I wanted to say that I could hardly have an opinion of it, not having read the blasted thing, but something took it out of my hands.

"Why are you telling me this?" I said.

He winked gallantly.

I went to the bathroom.

Twenty minutes later when I figured it would all be over, I came out. I was right; they were talking about chowders or clowders or fish parts or something. The trick of doing this is to insinuate yourself carefully into the group by stages in a dimmed-down sort of way so that the inevitable liberal in the group can't come up and apologize for the bad behavior of the first nut, because then you have the problem of whether or not to dress him down for not having come to your aid earlier, whereupon he gets a little snappish and says he thought that a woman fighting her own battles was what women's liberation was all about. Another way to avoid this is to eat a lot. I saw that Jean was attempting to slouch as disgustedly as possible in the kitchen (stomach out) because she does not like her father's friends. Her parents have very good, unimaginative food at their parties, which is a relief after you've been exposed to a lot of bad attempts at curry, or the kinds of things graduate students do under the romantic impression that nobody's ever cooked before. Jean's mother has a maid who comes in every day to clean up and everyone in the family (but Jean) thinks the maid is a very serious cross to bear because she talks a lot. I suspect the maid has crosses of her own. (She's white hill-people with bad legs: varicose veins and swollen ankles.) Jean's mother stayed home with her four children until the youngest was eleven, as was only right (she said); then when she went out to work after eighteen years she had, of course, to get household help. "My mother has too much energy," says Jean. There was the usual nervous discussion about Them (Blacks, who else?) in which Jean's father maintained with desperate, unhappy passion that They were better off than Black people in other parts of the world and the whole company (including me, I am sorry to say) jeered at him most cruelly; Jean's father is a kind of eccentric knicknack in his friends' eyes. They're liberals and they won't stand for anything biased or unfair. I have in me a demon who had slept all through the previous really rather personally painful exchange (I mean the MLA article) and which was now beginning to wake up—to keep it down I started talking with my female neighbor about the clothes you can't buy for summer any more, and the old trolley-cars (which we both remembered) with the woven sides that went half-way up. My mother's summer shoes used to be similarly woven, with some sort of holes in the straw-y fabric, and her rayon dress (the first synthetic) also had little patterns of holes. I used to think summer was made of little patterns of refreshingly aerated holes. Also putting away the winter drapes, if you remember, and the rug, and putting slipcovers on the furniture, although I do not know why anyone ever did or (for that matter) stopped. Mysterious. I love women—I mean I just decided that, talking to her; I mean women don't come up to you and go sneerk, sneerk, menstruation ha ha. You can have a simple, lovely conversation about 100% polyester double knit and what do they *think* they're selling for summer fabrics these days!—it's like astronomy, like zoology, like poetry—without taking your life in your hands, as I seem to do every time I talk to a man. The men, by the way, were deep in international politics (of a rather amateur kind) at the other end of the table. The one Continental thing Jean's parents do is to serve a good deal of wine with their formal meals, so I think my neighbor was getting a little zonked; she was telling about how it had been, going to a woman's college twenty years ago, that if you wanted to be a scholar you had to wear lisle stockings, Oxfords, and mannish suits or nobody would take you seriously. Wasn't it wonderful now (she said) that we could all be *feminine*? She said this over and over, like a life-raft. I said Yeah, I guess. Faculty wives (she teaches part-time—freshman courses) tend to dress for parties like a rather weird version of TV talk-show hostesses, as if they had tried but hadn't got it quite right—and this nice lady, my table-mate, was wearing a long red silk skirt slit up one knee and a white organdie blouse with ruffles down the front of it. Dangling ivory earrings, I believe. Very strange. I mean all those things that glittered and all that stuff *put* on her (on her face) and inside all that the real face, looking sad. She said *she* wasn't a woman's-libber, she wouldn't burn her bra, but with such a frightened look that I wanted to put my arms around her. Blonde hair carefully combed down her back (dyed). Not what you'd call freely blowing in the breeze, exactly (like in the ads) but that was the idea, I suppose. "Oh, that never happened," I said. "That was invented by the newspapers." (And this is so.) Then she began to tell me what a rotten life she had—at every faculty party there's a faculty wife who ends up with me in a corner, crying over what a rotten life she's had (but it's always a different woman)—and then when I started talking about babysitters, free time, husbands doing housework, etc., she said: "I have a very rich life. I love my husband and children," and retreated into the fruit salad. "What a beautiful child Jean is!" said my neighbor. "You know," she went on, "family life is not dying, as they say," and here, in an assumed tone of immense superiority, started to talk about how her children needed her because they were fifteen and seventeen respectively. "Yes, dear," I said; "Isn't the salad nice?" (Sometimes they begin crying at this stage.)

Don't imagine, she said, *don't imagine that anything I've told you indicates—is—the slightest—shows that I'm—means shows the slightest—*

"What are you two gabbing about!" cries her husband with uncharacteristic heartiness and jollity from the other end of the table.

"Patterns," I said.

"I think," said my neighbor, her chin *very* high in the air (and still spiffed, I am glad to say) "that women who've never married and never had children have missed out on the central experiences of life. They are emotionally crippled."

Now what am I supposed to say to that? I ask you. That women who've never won the Nobel Peace Prize have also experienced a serious deprivation? It's like taking candy from a baby; the poor thing isn't allowed to get angry, only catty. I said, "That's rude and silly," and helped her to mashed potatoes.

"*You* wouldn't know," said she, with a smirk.

"It's rude, Lily," I said in a considerably louder voice, "and if you go on in this way, I shall have to consider that you are both very foolish and very drunk. Eat your potatoes." Scenes bother ladies, you know. Also she thought her husband might be listening in. Do you know who her husband is?

The liberal!

"Phooey," said Lily dimly, into her plate. (Oh dear, but she had had a lot to drink!) "*You* can't catch a man."

"That's why I'll never be abandoned," said I. Fortunately she did not hear me. Did I say taking candy from babies? Rather, eating babies, killing babies, abandoning babies. So sad, so easy.

Something is changing within me. Did I mention my demon? It goes to sleep at its post sometimes, but it was back now and now I didn't mind it; when we got up for dessert and coffee in the living room (and then the screened-in back porch, for it was a hot night and everybody was sweating from having eaten so much) I decided I liked my demon. It has possibilities. Conscientious clawlets out, a-lert and a-ware, prowldy, prowldy, woman's best friend. Maybe I was a little drunk myself. Something in the back of my mind kept coming up insistently and I kept irritatedly shoving it away; I don't want to think of that now. Did you know that the Liberal is a tall, athletic type with everything except a straight backbone and the original Hartyhar is ginger-moustached, older, shorter, redder, a little plump as if he were going to burst his clothes, which are imitation British? He's one of those academic men who imitate English dress under the impression that—well, I don't know under what impression. It's idiotic, especially in summer. They're not such big deals; they're just fools. Oh, I know they're fools; I've always known. Stay with me, demon. Somebody started a discussion about the mayor we're all going to elect in the fall because we're politically conscientious (though his winning certainly won't change my life). I was asked what my politics were.

"Menstruation," I said, with a bit of a snarl.

"Oh come, come, come," says slick-and-suave, "I really do apologize for that, you know." (But he never looks sincere, no matter what he says; he always looks greasy and lying.)

"My politics," said I in a glorious burst of idiot demonhood, "and that of every other woman in this room, is waiting to see what you men are going to inflict on us next. That's my politics."

"Well, you can't get along without us, now can you?" says piggy, with a little complacent chuckle. This is my cue to back off fast-fast-fast—and Jean was looking at me from inside the living room—was it warningly? I couldn't tell. She was too far away to be anything but sibylline. I said crossly that they could all go stuff themselves into Fish Lake; it would be a great relief to me.

He twinkled at me. "Disappointed in love," he said.

I think he thought that I thought that he thought that I thought I was flirting. This is unbearable. I'm absolutely paralyzed.

"I can see that you like spirited wenches," said the obedient puppet who lives inside me.

Everybody roared appreciatively.

"What you don't understand," said our fake Briton (why do they always say this?) "is that I'm not against the women's liberation movement. I believe in equal pay for equal work. But surely you ladies don't need equality when you can wrap us around your little fingers, now do you?"

The Liberal was looking at me with his eyes shining, as if I were going to stand up and sing Die Walküre. Afterwards he will come up to me and say in a *very* low voice that he thinks I was *very* brave.

"Leave me alone," I said leadenly. I should never have started.

"Ah, but that's just what we don't want to do!" cried piggy. "We love you. What bothers us is that you're so oversensitive, so humorless, of course that's the lunatic fringe of the movement—I bet you thought I didn't know anything about the movement, didn't you!—but seriously, you've got to admit that women have free choice. Most women do exactly what they want."

"Just think," said someone else, "how much good the women of this community have done lobbying for a new school."

The demon got up. The demon said Fool. To think you can eat their food and not talk to them. To think you can take their money and not be afraid of them. To think you can depend on their company and not suffer from them.

Well, of course, you can't expect people to rearrange their minds in five minutes. And I'm not good at this. And I don't want to do it. It's a bore, anyway. Unfortunately I know what will happen if we keep on; I'll say that if we are going to talk about these things, let us please talk about them seriously and our fake Britisher will say that he always takes pretty girls seriously and then I'll say Why don't you cut off your testicles and shove them down your throat? and then I'll lose my job and then I'll commit suicide. I once hit a man with a book but that was at a feminist meeting and anyway I didn't hit him really, because he dodged. I have never learned the feminine way of cutting a man down to size, although I can imagine how to do it, but truth to tell, that would go against what I believe, that men must live up to such awful things.

Dead silence. Everybody's waiting. What do you do after you blow up, nitwit? I could already hear them twittering, "Didn't you notice? She's unbalanced." There's a solution to this problem. The solution is to be defeated over and over and over again, to always give in; if you always give in (gracefully) then you're a wonderful girl. I am terribly unhappy. I smiled and got up, and I made my way out in that ghastly way you must after a defeat, while Piggy-brit said something or other which I didn't even hear, thank God. Like being eight again on the playground; I will *not* let them see me cry. I walked through the living room and out the front door; after all, I can go back in another twenty minutes. I can ask to help Jean in the kitchen, to avoid all those others. My mother used to tell me not to hurt people's feelings, but what do you do if they hurt yours? But it's my own fault. The worst thing is that you can't kill that kind of man; I imagined very vividly hitting him with a plate or the punchbowl. Then I imagined pulling his ear off with my fist. I called him a shit-head and a stupid, filthy prick. I knocked him down. After I had sort-of hit the man with the book, I had trembled all day and cried. You can't kill them; they grow up again in your nightmares like vines. I thought I would feel better if I stepped out on the lawn and smelled the good night air, which doesn' t care that I'm crazy. Somewhere there is a book that says you ought to cry buckets of tears over yourself and love yourself with a passion and wrap your arms around yourself; only then will you be happy and free. That's a good book. I stood inhaling the scent of the ever-blooming roses on the corner of the lawn and thinking that I was feeling better already. God, had I been a liar when I'd said we ought to judge people as individuals? Of course not! I'd had a bad analyst—well, there's no guarantee. I'd had a nice, crazy, bruised husband. Well, he'd had a bad family. There's no reason to spend time with people you don't like. Jean doesn't like her father's friends, either (her mother is very quiet and doesn't initiate social things much). I said to my demon that there are, after all, nice people and nasty people, and the art of life is to cultivate the former and avoid the latter. That not all men are piggy, only some; that not all men belittle me, only some; that not all men get mad if you won't let them play Chivalry, only some; that not all men write books in which women are idiots, only most; that not all men pull rank on me, only some; that not all men pinch their secretaries' asses, only some; that not all men make obscene remarks to me in the street, only some; that not all men make more money than I do, only some; that not all men make more money than all women, only most; that not all men are rapists, only some; that not all men are promiscuous killers, only some; that not all men control Congress, the Presidency, the police, the army, industry, agriculture, law, science, medicine, architecture, and local government, only some.

I sat down on the lawn and wept. I rocked back and forth. One of those awful drunk downs. (Only I was sober.) I wouldn't mind living in a private world and only seeing my women friends, but all my women friends live in the middle of a kind of endless soap opera: does he love me, does he like me, why did he say that, what did he mean, he didn't call me, I want a permanent relationship but he says we shouldn't commit ourselves, his feelings are changing towards me, ought I to sleep with him, what did he mean by that, sex is getting worse, sex is getting better, do you think he's unstable, I'm demanding too much, I don't think I'm satisfying his needs, he says he has to work—crisis after crisis and none of it leading anywhere, round and round until it would exasperate a saint and it's no wonder their men leave them. It's so unutterably boring. I cannot get into this swamp or I will never get out; and if I start crying again I'll remember that I have no one to love, and if anyone treats me like that again, I'll kill him. Only I mustn't because they'll punish me. Certain sorrows have a chill under them, a warning-off from something much worse that tells you you'd better leave certain things unexplored and unexplained, and it would be best of all if you couldn't see it, if you were blind. But how do you blind yourself once you see enough to know that you ought to blind yourself?

It was at this point that I heard behind me a formal, balanced sentence, an Ivy Compton-Burnett sentence, hanging in the air in front of the house. The kind of thing written in letters of fire over the portals of the Atreidae. Such language!

It was in Jean's voice. It was elegant, calm, and very loud. The words "stupid prick" in it recurred several times.

She came up behind me in a great rush and flung her arms about me. It occurred to me that although we'd shaken hands and made those rather formal, ritualized cheek-kissings that one does, otherwise we'd never touched before. It was a bit startling. Also she's bigger than I am.

"Oh you good girl!" she cried. "Oh you splendid good girl!" She added, more conversationally, "Did you hear what I said?"

"But your mother—" I said. "Your father—"

"That!" said this unbelieving Valkyrie with scorn, and hugging me as if I had acted like a heroine, which you and I know I most certainly had not. "Look, Esther, I don't have to come here. If they want to keep up the family pride by having me visit once in a while, they treat me right. Otherwise I stay away." She laughed.

"A secret ally," I said.

"Oh," she said, "you should have seen their faces when I told them you were right!"

Her last words, she said, before she had informed the whole company that they were a bunch of cowards. ("You don't know the effect that has on the liberal types," she added, making a face.) Jean is an aristocrat who believes in good people and bad people (mostly the latter) but not in class warfare; I reminded her of this.

"Exactly," she said comfortably. "They're bad. They deserve to be told so. Besides, I already have my money for next year. My last year."

"You can cope and I can't," I said. Then I said, "I thought you weren't a feminist. Not really."

"I'm not," said Jean, squatting on the lawn and smiling at me. "I'm a me-ist."

"Let us," she added, with a look at the house and in a tone of profound disgust, "go somewhere else, for heaven's sake."

We went to Joe's and had a beer and French fries, sitting so we didn't have to face the television set directly. It went from a

Western to a hockey game to a fight. Then Olga Korbut, the Russian gymnast who is only 4' 10" high, came on and started doing beautiful and impossible back-flips; but just then one of the men from Jean's co-op waved to us and came over. He began talking earnestly about Jean's commitment to social revolution and Jean said lightly, "Oh, you'd be amazed at the number of things I'm not committed to," but he wasn't going to take it as a joke—which (unfortunately) reminds me of all the circumstances under which I have behaved in exactly the same way. He said again that he hadn't seen any evidence of Jean's being politically committed, and she said furiously that the next time she came out of the library with a fifteen-pound foreign-language dictionary, she'd drop her commitment on his foot. He said, "You're selfish." (Some of the things Jean is not entirely committed to in his opinion: Communism, Third World peoples, the workers, ecology, and organic foods. The one thing she is absolutely not committed to: white middle-class young men who suffer.)

I gathered X's shirt-front in one hand and brought us nose to nose. Oh I had cool! I said the following, which I am going to quote you in full because I am proud of it, very proud of it indeed, and it embarrassed him. Radicals shouldn't be embarrassed. It went like this:

"You a radical? Bullshit. Radicals are people who fight their own oppression. People who fight other people's oppression are liberals or worse. Radicalism is being pushed to the wall. Would you dare to tell Sawyer" (a Black acquaintance of his) "that he's selfish because he's committed to himself? Yet you tell us. Do you dare to tell a little country with bombs being dropped on it that it's selfish? Yet you dare to tell us. You're white, male, and middle-class—what can you do for the revolution except commit suicide? When the sharks start swimming around our raft, *you're* gonna get Daddy to send a helicopter for you; you could shave your beard and cut your hair and in five minutes go right back to the enemy. Can Jean cut off her breasts? Don't say it, pure soul. You a revolutionary! You just want to purge your sins. If you're still a revolutionary in ten years I'll eat this tablecloth."

Isn't that stunning? (Even if it wasn't *quite* as good as that.)

Then I added, for the poor thing looked as if it might speak, "No, don't say it. Go away gracefully. Anything either of us does now is bound to be embarrassing."

He said that he we couldn't make him leave because he had a right to be there, so I said *we'd* leave, but on second thought we didn't want to leave, so he'd better go because if he didn't I could do all sorts of unpleasant things, like shouting in my trained teacher-voice (current suburban children can't speak above a whisper), or wringing his nose (which hurts awfully and looks silly into the bargain), or yanking at his ears, or throwing water all over him, or hitting him, which I might not be good at but oh, would it be embarrassing. He got up.

"No," I said seriously. "Don't say it. Think again."

He went away.

I felt sorry for him. It's that tender, humane compassion you feel right after you've beaten the absolute shit out of somebody. I suppose if he feels so bad somebody must be doing *something* to him, but this, of course, is exactly what our walking Jesus Christs never admit. I could have mentioned this is my magnificent rhetorical performance, but it's a fact I cleverly concealed out of sheer brilliance.

Why does Jean look now as I looked before? Why did I look then as she looks now?

"Jean, dear," said I, "tell me about God," for religion is the one thing we really have in common. Jean's religion is this: that somewhere (or rather, everywhere) in the universe there is a fourth dimension, and that dimension is the dimension of laughter. Eskimos, finding themselves stuck in a blizzard for the fifth day, foodless, on a piece of ice insecurely fastened to the mainland, burst out laughing when that piece of ice finally moves out to sea, thus dooming them (the Eskimos or whoever they really are) to a slow, painful, and horrible death. They laugh because it's funny; Jean and I understand that. On the Day of Judgment, Jean says, when we all file past God to be judged, He will lean down and whisper into our ears the ultimately awful joke, the ghastly truth, something so true and yet so humiliating, so humiliating and yet so funny, that we will groan and rock back and forth and blush down to the bone. "I'll never do it again," (we'll say) "never, never. Oh, I feel awful." Then they'll let you into Heaven. There will be long lines of sinners giggling and snurfing and bending double with shame.

"What will Christ do during all this?" I said.

Jean said Christ was a liberal and would stand around looking sort of upset and helpless, saying, "Oh, Dad, don't."

I've talked of God as She. Perhaps it's the He-God who repeats the joke. The She-God *is* the joke.

But Jean had a toothache, a mental toothache. She didn't want to stay. It's a dreary subject, whom you outrank and who outranks you, and I pull rank on him and she pulls rank on them, and this plane leaves for Bergen-Belsen in fifteen minutes, not that we really murder each other, Heavens to Betsy, no, not yet.

Jean didn't like Joe's any more.

Leaning her silly, beautiful, drunken head on my shoulder, she said, "Oh, Esther, I don't want to be a feminist. I don't enjoy it. It's no fun."

"I know," I said. "I don't either." People think you *decide* to be a "radical," for God's sake, like deciding to be a librarian or a ship's chandler. You "make up your mind," you "commit yourself" (sounds like a mental hospital, doesn't it?).

I said Don't worry, we could be buried together and have engraved on our tombstone the awful truth, which some day somebody will understand:

WE WUZ PUSHED.

Many years ago, when I thought there was no future in being a woman, I awoke from a very bad dream and went into the bathroom, only to find that I had just got my period. I was living in a small New York apartment then, so there was barely room for me in the bathroom, what with the stockings hung over the railing of the bathtub and the extra towels hanging on the hooks I'd pounded into the wall myself. I stared at that haggard 2 A.M. face in the mirror and had an (imaginary) conversation with my uterus. You must imagine my uterus as being very matter-of-fact and down-to-earth and speaking with a Brooklyn accent (I grew up there).

LITTLE VOICE FROM DOWN BELOW: Look, I'm not doing anything. Whaddaya want from me anyway?

I lit a cigarette from the pack I kept on top of the toilet tank. (I used to smoke a lot in those days.)

LITTLE VOICE: If you're mucked up in the head, that's not my fault. I'm just doing the spring cleaning. You clean out the apartment once a week, right? So I'm doing it once a month. If you wanna be fertile, there's certain ways you gotta pay. It's like income tax. Don't blame me.

Silence. I smoked and brooded.

LITTLE VOICE: I want a hot water bottle.

So I got the sensible little thing its hot water bottle, and I went back to bed and fell asleep.

I accompanied Jean for days, looking sideways at her and admiring her romantic profile, her keen eyes, the large, fake, railroad-engineer's cap she wore in imitation of a famous French movie star in a famous French movie. I followed my shield-maiden all over campus as we rambled through libraries and gardens. I wanted to open doors for her. I do think Jean is one of the seven wonders of the world. My shrink once told me that I would stop envying and resenting men when I had made a satisfactory heterosexual adjustment, but I think he got it backwards. We had an awful fight about it. Jean and I sat in the hidden garden behind the art museum and told each other horror stories.

"...and, as any connoisseur of the subject might imagine, a disembodied Hand came creeping round the bed-curtains like a large, uncomfortable spider. Lady Letitia screamed—"

"—and screamed—" (said I).

"—and screamed—but not very loud because I have to finish the story. The Earl, awakened by he knew not what formless bodings, stumbled out of his room and down the great staircase—"

"—but quietly, because you don't want to wake anyone else up—"

"—where he was found dead the next morning, a look of nameless terror stamped upon his perfect British features.

Meanwhile, back in the pantry, a slithering, rugose tentacle investigated ranks upon ranks of jelly-jars. Could the pet octopus have got loose? Alas, it seemed not likely since—"

Oh, the numbers and numbers of slithering, rugose tentacles I've met in my time! And the squamous abominations and nameless cravings from beyond the stars and accursed heaps of slime in ancient, foetid cellars, and the opened crypts lit by hellishly smoking torches whose filthy punk (that's wood, lunkhead) give out an odor of the charnel house whilst succubi vanish into mouseholes in the fourth dimension (located in old New England attics) and strange figures celebrate blasphemous rites with unspeakable howlings and shocking sacrifices to nameless eidolons of hideous basalt mounted on...well, on Singer sewing machines, I suppose. And my eyelids sink in a luxurious, lovely droop. Why are horrors always nameless? Does that make them worse? It certainly puts you to sleep faster. The names things do have to put up with sometimes—for instance this secret garden (hidden behind the old museum, which was some trustee's mansion in 1875) is called the Emily M. Mapleson Planting after the lady who left it as a bequest to our institution. Poor woman! I would have called it Emily's Garden. For some reason every flower in it is white; at different times of the year different white blooms are potted in (though I've never caught anyone doing it; perhaps Ms. Mapleson endowed it with elves, too). Emily's Garden is completely hidden from the outside view by a dense stand of evergreens; inside are two stone benches, and in the middle of the flower beds a plaque with the name I've mentioned and a rather lumpish bronze faun with silly teeth. The whole thing is no more than fifteen feet across. At this time of year, in mid-August, very little is flowering; there's a lot of groundcover, small white blossoms (like Baby's-breath or Sweet William), with swaying Cosmos just inside the borders and a lot of dishevelled Phlox in the middle, shedding like mad. Someone has put a few Shasta daisies (which are— or look—greenish in the shade) behind the benches. It's not yet time for the Aster family and last week's white snapdragons have failed and been taken away to mourn themselves. Late summer is a difficult time for gardens because so

little happens. Jean has got to "a terrible slithering splash in
the old attic" and I tell her for Heaven's sake, how can you
splash in an attic?

"In the cellar," she says. "Besides, they keep an old washing
machine in the attic." Helpless laughter from both of us at the
idea of the Lurker from the Stars bobbling about in the family
laundry. I ask her will she finish the thing off, for goodness'
sake.

"All right, a great number of shots rang out and everyone
dropped dead. The end," said Jean.

It was very quiet in Emily's Garden. Flowers make no noise.
Beautiful little plant genitals swaying in the breeze and sur-
rounded by vast evergreens; earlier in the year yellow
hemlock-pollen had drifted on to the spring flowers, the
ground, the benches. Even the now-disgraced snapdragon
bells made no noise. I was trying to concretize all this "blasphemous," "rugose," "nameless" stuff in the person of a
clump of hysterical Phlox at my feet, each plant looking like a
mad prima donna: Ophelia, perhaps, scattering used-looking
white flowers in all directions. Phlox blossoms are insecurely
fastened to their stems at best, so the flower-spire always gives
the impression of letting its hair down. Phlossoms. The phlos-
soming Phlox. The phantasy of the phlooms of the Phlox.

I looked up into Jean's face, about to tell her about the
Phlooms of the Phlox, but I was dazzled. Absolutely dazzled.
All this happened before I had words for it, before I could
even identify it; I felt the blow, the astonishment, the thing-in-
itself. Something transmitted, something endured with a
gasp. Unspeakable. Unnameable.

Elves got your tongue? said the swaying white Cosmos.

"'Rugose' only means 'red,'" I said to Jean.

She agreed.

It's all right as long as it's nonsense, just fantasy. I'll understand in a moment. It's ridiculous to say that I'm in love with
Jean, because Jean is a woman, and besides she exasperates
me too much for that. I know her far too well. It's all fantasy
and admiration, just as the blooms in Emily M. Mapleson's
Planting are not Lucia di Lammermoor (a heroine of the
patriarchy who went mad when deprived of her lover, stabbed

her husband—with the overhand, or opera grip, not the proper underhanded tennis-racket one—and died, presumably from too many high C's). How can I giggle about Lucia and yet not be able to keep my eyes off Jean? It's all right if it doesn't mean anything. The memory of seeing her breasts silhouetted beneath her blouse went through me, went right through me, with such a pang that the horizon ducked as if I'd tried to hit it—ducked like a boxer while I clung to Emily M. Mapleson's cement bench because I was falling down. There's no excuse for it. I must make my heterosexual adjustment, as Count Dracula told me when together we chased the Big O, that squamous, rugose, slithery little man with his techniques and his systems and his instructions about what "wives" do for "husbands" and what "husbands" do to "wives"—what did he think *we* were doing, running after love with a butterfly net?

It's all right if I don't mean it. If I never tell Jean. If I never tell anybody. If I do nothing.

I accepted it on those terms.

What you do sordidly, in cellars.

"What?" said Jean. It seems that I had spoken aloud. She then informed me that she had already finished that silly horror story. I decided I must babble of something so that she would think I was behaving normally, while the sun shot arrows through my bones—although I do not look like a truck driver with a duck-tail haircut, do I?—while my sex radiated lust to the palms of my hands, the soles of my feet, my lips (inside), my clumsy, eager breasts, while they radiated it back to between my legs and I very obligingly thought I was going to die.

What is lust?

A permission of the will.

Jean began to talk about tenth-century Icelandic proper names—but that's all I heard, for she was walking in front of me and I watched her tapering back fit into the vase of her behind as if I'd never seen such a miracle before—which I hadn't, because I swear on my foremothers' bones that this is the first time since the age of twelve that I'd even thought of such a thing. And who doesn't, at twelve?

Count Dracula told me I was blocked. He told me I must

Try. How to Feel Lustful Against Your Will. He never told me how it goes in waves from your belly up to your chest, and then into your head, and then down again; when I felt nothing above the belly-button he seemed to think that was A-OK—the Lurker in *his* Attic was "genital insufficiency," which the ladies seemed prone to (said Count D.), the poor ladies who wanted a lot of all-over skin contact, he with his screw-driver or power-lathe approach.

"Are you sure you're all right?" said my suspicious friend, turning around and frowning with concern. "You look funny." Telepathy? Two can play at that game.

I told her I was very, very depressed. About the snapdragons.

We both screamed with laughter. I thought I could risk a look at her again, blazing with beauty with her Swedish chin and her beautiful behind, but again it happened: the pang, the blow, the astonishment.

Why, oh why didn't anyone tell me?

"Jean," I said, tottering at my own daring (but I won't tell her, oh no, not in a million years), "do you think one ought to go to bed with one's friends?" She looked at me with her wry look—beautiful, of course, for everything my friend Jean does is beautiful. And intelligent.

"With who else?" she said drily. "One's enemies?"

I tried to be a good girl, honest I did. I looked in the mirror and told myself I was bad. (This worked at the age of five, why not now?) But the self in the mirror loved me and laughed and blew kisses. I went about, cheerfully bawling popular songs in a very graceless manner; I sang "All Of Me, Why Not Take All Of Me" and "Love Is A Many Splendored Thing." I sang a bad country-and-western ballad with lots of twangy accompaniment between the lines, like this:

Ah hev a never-endin' luv fer yew,	(bloing, bloing)
And mah never-endin' luv is trew.	(bloing, bloing)
Ah luv yew so, whut kin ah dew?	(more bloing)
Ah hev a never-endin' luv fer yew.	(final bloing)

I'm lean, moody, prophetic. I'm aging well. (That's what the mirror tells me.) I want very much to sit in Jean's lap. Count Dracula and I have a long conversation about what is happening to me:

COUNT D: Now, Esther, let us discuss your perwersion.

ME: Sir, sirrah, ober-leutnant, sturmbannsfeuhrer, wherefore is it that you speak with a Viennese-Polish accent, whilst you are as Amurrican-born as you or I? Could it be that you have been reading too much Freud?

COUNT: No diwersionary tactics, Miss Frood. We must nip this abnormality in the bud before it flowers into something orbful. Do you realize that your present daydreams and style of life might lead to—gasp!—Lesbianism?

ME: Oh sirrah, tee hee, haw haw, you jest.

COUNT: I do not, indeed. What will you do when you are pointed at by The Phallic Phinger of Scorn? When your vile secret is exposed and your landlady throws you out of her apartment? When you lose your job? When rocks and sneers are thrown at you in the street?

ME: Who's going to tell them? You? I'll bust you in the fangs.

COUNT (complacently): Mordre wol out.

ME (mockingly): God will pun-ish.

COUNT: But seriously, Esther, don't you realize that your sexual desire for women is merely an outpouring of your repressed and sublimated desire for Mommy? How can I stand to think of my dear little girl, who might have a repressed (and therefore normal) desire for Daddy if she so chose—missing out on all the good things of life? You too could have a baby—

ME (aside): Little does he know that I could have a baby anyway.

COUNT: You could have a home in the suburbs, a floor to wax, a dear hubby all your own, a washing machine, a ouija board—·

ME (sotto voce): I think I *will* have a baby.

COUNT (unheeding): Of course I know you have an automobile already, Esther, but think what an old, cheap automobile it is. It's the wrong make. You could have a nice, new, expensive automobile if you were heterosexual, especially if you were heterosexual with the right sort of man, i.e. men who have high salaries, like stock exchange brokers. Men make so much more money than women do. Think, Esther! all this and penis, too. But your prefer squalid, inconclusive embraces in basements, disgusting scenes with big, fat, low-income women in ducktail haircuts—

ME: What's wrong with being big and fat and having a ducktail haircut? What's good for Marlon Brando is good for the nation!

COUNT: Yes, you prefer doing things like in *Esquire* or *Playboy*—only backwards—all this instead of mending your hubby's sox and seeing the love shine thru his eyes.

(He thinks for a minute. This business about *Esquire* and *Playboy* is obviously not getting to me, perhaps because it has nothing to do with me. He thinks that I think that he thinks that I think that I *really do* read girlie magazines. Then he finds it.)

COUNT: Esther, have I ever lied to you?

ME: Yes.

COUNT: Then listen to me now. Don't you realize that your desire for women is merely a repressed and sublimated desire for men? If you could get men, you wouldn't want women and we could forget all about this dreadful nonsense. You're not a real homosexual. Real homosexuals have horns. Your pseudo-homosexual desire for your friend springs from an insist complex whereby the great mother-figure stands at the doorway of your libido, making nasty, negative gestures and warning you back from the promised land of your father's womb.

ME: My father's—?

COUNT: If only you were able to realize that the penis is equivalent to the breast and the breast to the penis, you would understand that the great reality of normal sexual intercourse (which includes fellatio) lies in its ability to simultaneously allow the male to express his own maleness and the female to possess the male's maleness through her passive receptivity of his penis, thus transcending her own receptivity-oriented passivity (or passivity-oriented receptivity) and for the moment making the two one. And that one is the husband. People who suck each other off with their mouths or fingers are evading this great, primordial identity crisis (in which everybody becomes male) and remaining their sexually undifferentiated, irresponsible, pathologically pleasure-seeking selves. How do they know what kind of shampoo to use? What kind of deodorant? What color of comb? In such terrible cases a male might put on a flowered Band-aid or a female a shirt that buttons from left to right instead of from right to left. I might wake up one morning and find that my wife had bought for my birthday a belt with daisies embossed upon it. The heavens would fall!

ME: That is a better birthday present than strychnine, Count D, which otherwise your poor wife might assuredly get for you. Count D., Count D., I hereby dub thee not Count Dracula but Cunt Dracula. Come back, oh D., to the womb, come back to the head, come back to the cunt and fingers and feet which once called thee forth. You died long ago in reality; so what is not-me I hereby reject and throw out with the weekly garbage; what is me I re-appropriate.

Go away.

HIS PARTING SHOT: Esther, you are *bad* (because you don't like men).

Ah! that's a weak spot. I don't. But if what I feel for Jean is a substitute, then I had better never meet the real thing because I would certainly die from it. As it is, every time I have to wipe myself after going to the bathroom I bend double. Years ago, after our group therapy time was over, we would go to a coffee shop in the East seventies of Manhattan, a district full of embassies, of private schools, of luxury high-rise apartment buildings, one of the most expensive neighborhoods in any city in the world. Here Dr. D. had his office, despite the cost (for which we middle-class white people paid, even though we loathed writing copy for catalogs or putting out industrial newsletters) so every Thursday night after the post-mortem we would go and have "coffee"—this means hamburgers, pastries, late dinners for some, what-have-you. I liked these gatherings. I didn't like the sessions themselves; no matter how they went I didn't want to be there. Every week the woman who was afraid of staircases came in to report that she had gone up and down two steps or she hadn't and we commended her or blamed her; every week the man whose marriage was breaking up came in and told us how he was "working at the relationship" and we said Good for you. And every week for three years a little voice inside me said *Get out of here!* although I could never explain it. I liked the people. It was like that book on the power of positive thinking: *Every day in every way I am getting better and better.* There seemed to be no way to measure anything except by the book. Sometimes people in psychoanalysis were really cured and got normal—although there was no way for them to tell when they were normal, the doctor told them, I guess—and then (presumably) you just stopped coming because you Measured Up. Nowadays "relationship" is a euphemism for fucking or having a love affair, but then it meant something different, something grim, hard, central, and unrewarding, something you had to do anyway, whether you wanted to or not. You had to *work* at it. My husband, to the intuitive marrow of his bones, knew it was bad.

"How do you know when you're happy?" I said once.

They said impatiently that they weren't talking about that and besides of course you knew. The doctor added that a bag of heroin could make you ecstatically happy, if you wanted to function at such a low level. That sounded fine to me and I thought about it quite seriously, but in the end was scared away by the law (and my own inexperience).

I liked the coffee shop; that was where we really talked.

One night a new patient showed up: a cute ugly woman with a huge hooked nose and a receding chin who knew (she said) that if she'd only been born beautiful, she wouldn't have any "problems." Beauty was what mattered in this world.

"Oh, no, it's not important," we said with one voice—imagine, we in our high heels, nylons, girdles, wigs, padded brassieres, make-up, false eyelashes, painted fingernails, tipped and permanent-waved hair, and costume jewelry!

I never came back. Oh not melodramatically, not like that, but within a few months. It was an odd kind of religious cult like the Flat-Earth people or the Shakers; in a hundred years they will still be sitting around the coffee shop (it will still be

1963, it will still be the most expensive part of the world) waiting for the tooth fairy to zap down from the ceiling and endow them with the suburban substitute for bliss. Just as the suburbs are a bad imitation of the country and I and my husband were bad imitations of—well, would you believe angels? I do not mean to make light of the suffering, which was real enough and which at least brought us all face-to-face with something real, whatever it was and however frightening it might have been—but oh the muddle, the mystification, the nonsense, the earnestness, the silliness of the whole wretched business! It was without dignity, courage, or sense. It helped with some things—the gross things—if there'd been no re-turn at all, how could the doctor have stayed in business?— but all the same it reminds me of nothing so much as Ravel's "Bolero," which is the middle-brow substitute for music, that ghastly mock-Spanish piece you hear on every Muzak-be-dongled elevator; it and the elevator and the people in the elevator go round and round to infinity without ever getting anywhere, like a snake eating its own tail.

I hope somewhere they've all gotten out of 1963 and are thinking the same things about me.

I used to go home futilely to my sad, mad (but never bad) husband—who knew his own sickness too well to meddle with it—and admire his broad, knotted back, the muscles in his shoulders and arms, his lovely vulnerable belly, that pelvic crease of Greek scuplture that comes out in a man only when he stands on one leg, his funny little round-flat ass, his rubba-ble, bristly chin, that indescribable line from rib to hip, so subtle and so different from a woman's. Men have straight knees and elbows; women's go in. He would stand—wistful and banana-flowered—and I'd say tiredly over and over again (to an absent Dr. D.)that I had no troubles with sex, only with men, and that my trouble with men did not come from what was between their legs but from what was between their ears. My husband envied me my brain, that Bear of Little Brain. But I cannot cannot think of myself as the Nut Brown Maid or the Pretty Lady, truly I can't. And we only multiplied each other's angry clinging, he and I.

An awful thought:

What if Jean...won't?

I had two dreams that night and woke up scared; in one I was falling—nothing to see, just the sensation—and somebody giggled and told me, "You're in free fall." In the other I was very sick, being taken to the hospital on a stretcher and feeling so awful that I started to pray to get well, but that made me feel more helpless; so I prayed only that She might grant me endurance. That's all. "Give me my Self," I said. Then I woke up, with a sense of the dream over and (along with the fading of the dream) the sense of something being over for good. That's all the guilt I ever felt. I think I had it out somehow that night; it's like going through an electric fence where the worst point is just before you touch it and your nerves jump, but once you go through, it's O.K. I thought in my innocence: *Now I can be friends with men.*

Another marvelous discovery, in one of my waking periods at about 4 AM, a vision of the local Howard Johnson's (East of the campus, on the superhighway) full of healthy, comely young women. *There are others besides Jean!* For the first time in my life I felt free. In fact, I felt perfectly wonderful.

So I went happily back to sleep.

Jean came over for breakfast the next day, bringing some inferior lox, which is the only kind you can get in a small town like this. We ate it and made a face. I was wildly excited. I finally got up and did an imitation of Jean's last—latest?—boyfriend who was somewhere in Canada slaving away at a doctoral thesis.

"Absent lovers are the best kind," she said.

I can't wait. Can you?

The trouble is, if I make a pass at Jean or tell her anything, she'll just push me away. It'll ruin our friendship. And suppose she tells someone? (Though I don't think she'd do that.) It would be awful to have to have such suspicions. My kitchen had never seemed friendlier. We sat and talked about one thing and another—she was telling me nasty, funny stories about her professors (my colleagues!) and I had to decide there was nothing I could tell Jean, even though I'm looking over her shoulder at her math textbook (a course she's taking just for fun). I've pulled my kitchen chair so close that I can smell her, which makes me want to cry.

I will have to keep it a secret.

Unhappy. Miserably unhappy. Why? Because people do not do things like that in reality. Reality doesn't allow it. In books or movies or maybe newspapers, yes, but real life is not like that, and in real life if I were to throw my arms around my friend and kiss her, she would only wonder at my madness; she'd say, "Esther, stop it!" very sharply, and the heavens would re-form; reality—in which, by the way, I have as considerable a stake as anyone else—would simply remain itself. If I ever try anything I will be struck dead from on high anyway. (Some of the other things real people just don't do, according to my family: get divorced, become drug addicts, murder someone, kill their children, kill themselves, expose themselves in subways, get raped, fail in business, go mad.) So I can't do it. Of course I can't.

Clumsily I put my arms around her, twice-clumsily I kissed her on the neck, saying hoarsely, "I love you." (Which was something of an over-simplification, but how are you going to explain it all?)

She went on reading.

She blushed delicately under me, like a landscape, I mean her neck, she just turned red, it was amazing.

Reality tore itself in two, from top to bottom.

"Jean," said I, not believing my ears and eyes, "do you really—" but I guess she did! because she continued to pretend to read, only reddened like a tide, a forest, an entire planet. You don't ask the whole world if it's really doing what it's doing. I felt her skin get hot under my mouth. She closed her book deliberately, turned to me, and put her arms around me. *People* get divorced, *people* kill, *people* go mad. Saying I loved her might not have been so untrue, really—well, here was something worth dying for! When I think of those times that I did it to oblige, or because it was my duty, or to get affection, or because I couldn't refuse, I am ashamed. When I say "dying for" I mean the poems and the stories, the jokes, the obsessions, the terror, the wonder. I am dreadfully a-shamed of my past.

We sat back and looked at each other (frightened) at the same moment. Not because it was wrong but because it was an overcharge, like the copper wire you unwittingly overload and it's going urp! help! eek! aargh! oop! (in Wire) and you don't even know why the poor thing is jumping and twitching so. Better if calmer. Men think that once you admit your desire you have to fall down and fuck on the floor right-away, but women know better; I helped her to some inferior lox and A & P cream cheese and she did the same for me. We munched away at our bagels together. Suddenly she laughed and choked on hers.

"Shame on you," she said, "making love to someone you've known for only three years!"

I said, "Well, I can't get you pregnant, can I?" feeling very daring.

We laughed until we cried, partly out of nervousness. We were both (I think) rather wary of touching each other again. So much more is at stake now. Jean went back to explaining her book, only she reached out now and again and stroked my hand. I was blind, deaf, overwhelmed. I kept wanting to put my fingers through the central hole of the last bagel because it struck me as such an extraordinarily good joke; there was a sort of divine giggle somewhere in the room.

"You don't mind?" I cried suddenly.

She caressed my hand again. The nearest part of Jean to me (once she sat back and continued reading) was her foot, for she had crossed her legs and one foot kept advancing toward me and then retreating. Now feet are not as compromising as hands and not so close to the person, so I grasped Jean's individual, very expressive foot and admired her arch, which is so much higher than mine. I was terrified. (She looked pleased and a little embarrassed.) I explained about feet and that I was not a foot-fetishist, really, but hands were too vivid for me right then, so she let me hold on to her ankle; I kept imagining that she would change her mind at any moment, that she was merely being charitable, that she was intimidated, that she'd "mind."

I know too well what can really be going on when women are silent.

We talked about how everybody was bisexual, and how this was only the natural result of a friendship, and how we had better take our time, and then—like virgins—began to whisper, "When did you first—?" and "When did you—?" "I knew instantly by the way you looked at me," she said, and I turned red from head to foot at the thought of being so transparent, in veils and waves of heat.

Jean "screwed" the last bagel with her forefinger, looking very severe and haughty.

I gingerly picked up the ends of her dark hair, where they lay on her shoulder. It was like picking up something living, with nerves in it, and it used to annoy me when men told me I should grow my hair. Though I would never tell anyone what to do.

"I have to go," she said.

Relief.

"My job," she said. "You know." (She has a part-time job at the University library, checking out books or something.)

"You won't—" I said.

"I'll tell *everyone*," said my friend, making a face, and I was really ashamed. I knew and she knew—and she knew that I knew—that really it was too much and we'd better both recover a little. Better to be calmer. She said she would come that night—no, tomorrow night, but tonight come down to the co-op and help bake a cake if I wanted—she would turn up tomorrow night with some pot.

"It hurts my tonsils," I said. (But the idea was to keep from getting scared or anxious.) "Poor little thing," she said, and then bent down and kissed me on the mouth for a few seconds. Oh dear. They never tell you your clitoris is connected right to your stomach. I was terribly frightened that sex would be just as bad with her as it had always been with a man but at the same time I didn't care because it was such a glorious opportunity to fail, you see. I didn't really care. (I think I had better stop saying "really.") But if it turned out badly, what would I do then? I kissed her back on her velvety cheek.

Women's faces are covered with fine, almost invisible down. I said to myself that whatever happened, we'd still be friends, but I knew that was the talk of a fool; I didn't want to be friends. I didn't actually know what I wanted, being too much involved in her individual odor, and the smoothness of her skin, and her heavy, utterly lovely behind, to care about what had not yet happened. I kissed Jean on the cheek and said a trembly good-bye.

And staggered to the bedroom, kicked off my shoes mechanically, sat down on the bed. Pulled the curtains to, pulled down my pants, reached in the bottom drawer of the bureau for the vibrator.

A little voice cried, *You'll wear yourself out!*

But ah, that was impossible.

I didn't go to the co-op that night because my soul was already in too many pieces. Spent that day and the next wandering around: gardens, swine pens, the lamb barns with the lambies and their mommas (I was sobbing a little at everything because it was all so sweet). Just up and down the usual goldgreen lawns and under the lovely trees with their dark-goldgreen shadows, and some day we will all go the the great Multiversity in the sky. Beamed at all the men in the street. By 6 P.M. was convinced she wouldn't come, but every time I heard footsteps on the stairs I jumped. Something about keeping windows open (in the summertime) makes electric light very bright indoors. When she did come I was in the living room dusting the tables and didn't even hear her knock until she repeated it (Jean almost beats doors down). I had the weirdest fancy that Rose (you remember Rose; she's buried way back on page 1) was sitting in the shadows outside the lit circle of the living-room lamp. I walked from the dark room into the lit one, a progress to which all creation moves, one of those moments in which the shape of your house or your life takes on all the meaning in the world. I opened the door with no nerves at all, and Jean waved a bottle of wine at me. She's old-fashioned, she's decided, and doesn't like pot. It felt like any other visit. What's the etiquette for this sort of thing? I haven't tried to get drunk for love-making in years, but this is going right back to adolescence, so we solemnly took two glasses of medicine (feh) and then I ruined it by remembering a pound of ice cream I had in the freezer, which of course we had to share, more or less.

"I can't make love; I'm too full," said she.

I stroked her hand, then her arm. I put my arm around her and kissed her on the cheek.

"Do you want to?" I said. She nodded. We went into the living room and carefully pulled the curtains shut, then dragged a quilt from the bedroom. There isn't enough room on a single bed; besides, I like to feel that my whole house is my home. We put the wine on the floor near the quilt and lay on our stomachs, fully clothed. There is this impalpable barrier between everyday life and sex, perhaps to be connected up with that lack of etiquette I spoke of before; anyway there's some sort of gap you have to jump with your eyes shut, holding your nose (so to speak) as if you were jumping into water. I remembered, with fear of exactly what, I can't specify—that Jean is, after all, twelve years younger than me. Before we brought in the quilt I had trotted into the bedroom and brought out my vibrator, hiding it shyly between the couch cushions because it is really a gross little object, about eight inches long, made of white plastic and shaped like a spaceship. Contrary to popular belief, most women use vibrators on their outsides, not their insides. Unfortunately the batteries are wearing out and instead of going bzzzz it just rattles—the truth is I'm afraid Jean will find it repulsive or possibly that she will find me repulsive. She's down to her slip by now. I've always assumed I was reasonably good-looking— to men—but why should a woman have the same standards? Jean has finally taken off her clothes and so have I; to me she looks beautiful but very oddly shaped; I suppose there's the unconscious conviction that one of us has to be a man and it certainly isn't me. Jean says she wants to put a record on the hi-fi but I don't because it's too distracting. So she bursts into angry tears. I put my arms around her and rock her back and forth, which kept me from looking at her, so although she might have still looked odd (it was wearing off) she felt beautiful. Who doesn't look odd? Men look odd. God looks odd. We smooched a little, then put a record on the player (I don't remember what. Baroque?); then lay down and necked a little more, less timidly. I love Jean. She's a vast amount of pink-ness—fields and forests—but with my eyes closed it feels more to scale and it's nice. The way you measure the genuine-ness and goodness of an experience is this: what does it do to reading an ordinary magazine? If *Life* looks inexplicably silly to you, then life is doing its stuff. This is what I use myself and I recommend it (undoubtedly there are other tests). My friend is snowfields and mountains. Another world. Her odor (ev-eryone has a particular, own smell) is a complicated key, one among millions. I don't understand her. For example, I don't know why she's still upset now—so I said, "Oh, phooey, turn over and I'll give you a back rub." Phooeys we doubt ever got phooeyed. She lay mistrustfully on her stomach and I knelt between her legs, gaily pounding away at her shoulder blades, very professional though I don't know a massage from a message. So soft, so soft. Back-rubs are sneaky, low-level trickery because there's something in our mammalian ances-try that signals Good good good when your back is rubbed and you wouldn't dream of not being trustful (like scratching a dog's ear or rubbing under a cat's chin). It's taking advan-tage. After I had busily kneaded her shoulders for a while, I sneaked down to the small of her back and started kissing her neck; she said, "This isn't fun for you, Esther, is it?"

"Oh no, not a bit," I lied. And slid down to the rose between her legs. That's exactly what it is. Amazing. (Medieval stories.) I have the advantage of knowing where everything is and more or less how to do it. And feeling the strangest sympa-thetic pangs. Besides, you cannot bite men's backsides because they haven't any. Jean began to breathe hard, which made me want to cry; I kissed her on the neck where I know that sensitive place. To be the cause of so much pleasure to some-one else!—as the book says, *to make a difference*. I knew that when Jean came, I would burst into tears.

"No—wait a minute—stop!" she said, rolling on her side and angrily pushing me away. She's very fair-skinned. From neck to groin my friend was covered with pale-red spots like an interesting variety of measles; I had never seen what the book calls "the sex rash" before. You know, just before climax. Utterly fascinating. You can only see it on very fair-skinned women and Jean is the eighteenth-century Irish ideal: dead-white skin, blue eyes, black hair. "Stop," she said. "I can't feel anything," she said. Wild roses and milk. The first time I came with a man (fooled you, didn't I? I bet you thought I never came with a man) I shouted "I can't! I can't get there, God damn it!" and proceeded to go into internal waves that surprised me because I thought you lost your mind when you did it. And there I was, thinking away as usual.

"Oh, Jean!" I said. She stalked angrily into the kitchen—to the window that was hidden (thank Heaven) by the branch of a tree—she drank a glass of water and came back into the living room. For those of you I am confusing by the "internal" in "internal waves" (above) I will tell you my own, recently-developed theory of sexuality, proven by years of experimental masturbating: i.e. you feel your climax most whenever you are being most stimulated. This opens surprising fields of research to those of us with suckling infants or three hands or other situations like that. Honest.

"I guess I can't," said Jean. "Or I don't want to. I mean I do want to but I suppose I can't—can I—if I'm behaving like this."

"If you don't want one, I don't want one," said I promptly. I thought *Behave any way you like. Stand on your head. Keep your clothes on. Make it with the electric toaster.* If I had to choose between always pleasing her but never myself and always pleasing myself but never her—well, I'd choose the former. At least for a while. I can always please myself afterwards. An orgasm is an orgasm, but how often is there a Jean?

"Never mind," she mumbled. "I never come with anyone."

Now this is really surprising, considering how many men she's been with. I suppose this is the time to whip out the vibrator and attack her with it, but somehow I have doubts about the whole proceeding. I think we began this wrong.

I tell her so. There should be no failure and no success.

Blushing very deeply, she asked me if she could do something. I said yes, of course. She averted her face and moved my hand on to her rose (sorry to be so kvetchily sentimental).

"Let me—ah—um—do it myself."

"Oh my goodness yes, is *that* all!" I cried. Trying to memorize the motion, an odd sort of diagonal one. Jean seems to like things done lightly.

She came in the usual way about three minutes later, not very satisfactorily, it seemed to me. She said I couldn't put my mouth down there because she hadn't had a bath for days. I said that sounded reasonable to me, although we might be wrong. She said her wrist hurt, and rubbed it. Then I lay down and Jean gave *me* a back rub and I was hung up on the edge of it forever. Finally, with not much satisfaction, I flipped over.

"That was awful!" said Jean, sitting up, tears in her eyes.

"Well," said I reasonably, "you know what they say in Swedish movies about the first time."

"What do they say in Swedish movies?" (rather sharply)

"Oh, dear, I don't know."

We sat for a while, had a glass of wine, and then began to cuddle. The formalities were over. (Thank goodness.) She kissed me and whispered to me that I was beautiful. I blew in her ears. I fulfilled a daydream of twenty years' standing and nibbled along her hairline, under her temples and around her ears. We lay on the quilt and got mildly potted, feeling—as is usual, I think, with people who take off their clothes—that nudity is the only pleasant state. The living room was a garden. We locked big toes and had a toe fight, then began to throw couch pillows at each other, but stopped guiltily when we knocked over my floor lamp.

"My big toes are bigger than your big toes!" hissed Jean, raking her toenails up and down my back.

"Ooooo!" I said. "Oo, I like that."

"She likes that muchly," said Jean.

Now what is the trouble? That sex doesn't commit you to anything, in spite of our tradition about it? That love doesn't give you a code of behavior? I think so. She could go away now and never come back. I saw already what the pattern of my love affair would be—worrying each time she was away, relieved each time she came back—or does that mean that Jean and I don't really love each other? Anyway, it's awful.

Jean got up and said Oh feh, she had to go. She put on her clothes regretfully and I put on mine; we rooted in the ice-cream container for the rest of the ice cream (Hail, Hearth and Home! Hail, O Great Food Goddess!). Then Jean went to the door. We said in unison:

"When will I see you again?"

A great relief, after years of being the only one to say it! I can't come to see her because of the co-op gang and Stupid Philpotts (though we could tie him to a peg on the back lawn if we had to) but there wouldn't be enough privacy in the co-op, though Jean has brought men there many times before. There's a difference. She kissed me on the edge of the chin and I watched her as she went downstairs, swaying like a snake standing on its tail. The Snake of Wisdom? Something embodied. Jean will surprise me some day and perhaps not nicely; there's the chill of finding out that I didn't know her as well as I thought, that there's something in her sexuality, even, that I didn't know about. Though I like it that she never came with a man, I love it that she came with me, however awkwardly, and I will love it no matter what she uses: my hand, her own hand, my glass paperweight with the private snowstorm over the New England Church (with the spire, kiddies). As the real Jean waned, the mythical part of Jean came back into my kitchen, flooding the waxed floor and the refrigerator and the little study I'd fixed up in the kitchen around the corner of the L; I tasted Jean, saw Jean, thought Jean, breathed Jean. The Jean I can keep in my head.

Bonny, bonny Jean.

George Eliot never ended her books properly. There's so little for heroines to do; they can fall in love, they can die. As the story begins, you wonder whether the heroine will be happy, but by the middle of it you're beginning to wonder if she will be good. Such is George Eliot's sleight-of-hand, i.e. cheating. We still think this way a hundred years later. I've been reading wretched-housewife novels written by women and they all end the same way; either the awful husband has a mysterious change of heart (off-stage) on the last page but one

or the wife thinks: Yes, but I really loved him so it was all right.
You would not believe the suffering and wretchedness in
these books. (And one of the characters is called Sophia, too,
which means Wisdom.) I spent two Jean-less days reading
these books and making marginal notes for some article or
other I was going to do next winter if I ever got around to it,
and then, like the heroines of these stories, I had a great
"realization," a pious illumination (they're always having
these, like their children really love them or they adore housework or they are really happy even though their husband ties
them to a newel post and beats them with a goldfish). Pro-
gressing by a series of flat denials of the evidence. My pious
illumination was that I did not want to do the article. But
everything in print is sacred, as we all know, including this
sentence. All words are sacred. (Unless written by a computer,
in which case the *computer* is sacred.) Some astonishing things
are sacred, really; thus we have the Pain Goddess and the
Sleeping-late-in-the-morning Goddess, the Trip Troll (who
makes the transmission fall out of your car fifteen miles from
your destination), and the Mayonnaise Deity, who presides
over gourmet cooking. Love is like sleeping late in the morning; you dive down through layer after transparent layer,
utterly content, farther and farther until you reach the sea
floor. But it's bottomless.

Waiting for Jean is pleasant: one anticipates her arrival.

Waiting for Jean is useful: perceptions are sharpened.

Waiting for Jean is educational: it teaches you that even
good things must be waited for.

Waiting for Jean is fortunate: that she will come at all makes
you feel blessed.

Waiting for Jean is exasperating: I can't wait much longer.

On the superhighway at night, doing sixty-five in my old
rattletrap; the wet, cloverleaf roads twist and turn under the
city lights like shining black snakes. It's just rained: brilliance
and darkness. I'm coming home from the art museum in a
town sixty miles away.

The world belongs to me. I have a right to be here.

Two days later, by mutual agreement, Jean came "just to visit." She came trotting up my stairs—or rather, dragging behind her the stately hem of a long, mauve-paisley dress. She always puts on long skirts and her shades when she wants to go in disguise. I sat with my feet curled under me, timid as a mouse, on my corner of the couch (where I was prepared to sit until Doomsday, if necessary) while Jean retailed gossip. Her gossip has one extraordinarily redeeming feature: she makes it all up. None of it is ever true. In the middle of an impossible detail about something the Dean's wife had said to the sales-girl, she looked at me long and hard and then narrowed her eyes, for I had cleverly drawn the curtains *before* she came. Just in case.

Then she took off her sunglasses and smiled at me, so that tears rose to my eyes. She unhooked her dress (home-made so no zipper) and let it drop to the floor, then with crossed arms shucked her slip and did a little victorious dance around the room, waving the slip in the air. We took off all our clothes, very soberly, and then had a cup of tea, sitting politely on the couch, naked; I went into the kitchen to fetch it in my bathrobe. We looked each other over and I showed Jean the mole on my hip; so she lifted her hair and showed me the freckles on the back of her neck. We compared our "figures" like little girls. We sat on the two ends of the couch, our knees up, feet to feet, and talked about the ecstacies and horrors of growing breasts at twelve, of bouncing when you ran, of having hairy legs, of being too tall, too short, too fat, too thin. There is this business where you think people end at the neck; then gradually as you talk, as we talked, as we reconstituted ourselves in our own eyes—how well we became our bodies! how we moved out into them. I understood that she felt her own ribs rise and fall with her breathing, that her abdomen went all the way into her head, that when she sat, she felt it, I mean she felt it in herself, just as I did. Until she looked—as she had felt to me before—all of one piece. Why is it impossible to talk about women without making puns? When you fuck someone, you are fucking with their eyes, too, with their hair, with their temples, their minds, their fingers' ends. (If we didn't wear clothes all the time we'd see personality all over, not just the face.) We sat side by side, holding hands and quite naked; then Jean put her arms around me and it felt so good that it made me stammer. Such astonishing softness and everything shaped just right, as if thirty years ago we had been interrupted and were only now resuming. I'd been worried, but it turns out to fit some exact shape in your head that you never knew you had, fits it with the perfection of a Swiss watch. As close as we blurry human beings can ever come to instinct. I had been worried about Jean, as I said, but now I didn't care, although I think she disliked the awkwardness of having to break apart in order to get up and go into the bedroom. I stroked her back to let her know I would do anything for her, set fire to the rug if she wanted, lean out the window in my skeleton, make a gift to her of all my insides, my pulsations, the electricity in my hair, the marrow of my bones. That's what they mean when they say your bowels yearn; something tries to move out through your skin. We lay down on the bed in each other's embrace but didn't do much; only I tried to explain how lovely it was for her to have long hair. She stopped me. "I don't mean to be sexist about it," I said; "It's just fortunate." It came to me as an inspiration, an astonishingly fine and surprising idea, that we should fuck each other now, for the excitement (although spread all over) did seem to be centering in one particular place and I was so beside myself with aching that I thought she must be too. And I must say the only disadvantage to its being Jean was that there weren't more arms. Anyway at the end you don't care if you are fucking a rhinoceros; you just want to go on and do it. She half did it and I half did it, moving against her hand, and because Jean knows what a woman feels she didn't stop at that moment but a little after, as soon as I had stopped. Then she said, "Hey, I took a bath this time," so I slid down and very cleverly (I read this in a book) sucked at her, this being something I would never think up all by myself because you can't very well practice on yourself, now can you? And we tried a little of this and a little of that, Jean being as inexperienced this way as myself, until we ended sitting up in bed with Jean in front of me, my left arm around her waist and my right hand between her legs, a very beautiful, statuesque pose.

I think the other takes practice. She came once a little bit but told me to keep on, which I did; she came again, awesomely. Like someone who's speaking in tongues, crying out, seeing visions.

"I'm noisy," she said. "I'm sluttish."

"Oh, do it again," I cried admiringly, "do it again!"

"Don't want to," said Jean.

"I hope I feel like an armchair," I said. I think what I always missed about men was breasts. Jean's are the usual shape—don't laugh, I mean they're not conical, the way some of us are—round enough, small enough; pulled down by gravity to be fuller underneath. She has one oddity; light circlets of hairs round her aureoles. Dreadfully sexy. How odd, to carry these empty milk cartons in front of us for sixty years, whether we use them or not. I think my own body has imperceptibly got to be some kind of standard for me; yet it was fascinating to see her so different. Not a line of her was imperfect. My bowels yearned with gratitude because I wanted to give her something, not for any reason, but for my own relief, for something that wanted to transfer itself out of me. My true love hath my heart and I have hers. Nothing I can name. This may simply have been a second grand idea that we should do it again, but at this point Jean got up and went into the bathroom in my sleazy pink rayon kimono (this is not my bathrobe because I own both).

"Madama Butterfly," I said.

When she came back, she sat down on the bed and started putting on her shoes. I said, "You're not going!"

She gave me a look which I recognized, having once been on the other side of the fence myself.

"I'm not?"

"Oh, of course you are," I said, "but please, please, don't. Please stay."

"I want to think about it," said my friend. She began to put on her underwear. This is the part of the movie or TV special where he speaks to her authoritatively and she obeys, or he tells her how she's got to be honest, so she bursts into tears and reveals her problem, which he then solves. But you and I know better; I'm not going to give Jean an excuse to pick a quarrel with me. And I didn't even try to look forlorn and waif-like; I was much too happy. And I could think of nothing except her. I begged her to wait until I had dressed so I could accompany her to the door, so she did. And I did. We both got decent. Standing at the door with no premonitions, waving goodbye as if we'd been having a late tea, with our clothes on all the time, quite respectably, in as false a position as possible. I saw her descend the stairs, me shutting my own door before she reached the bottom and went into the street. There would be something too final about the other way. I sat at the kitchen table, not to think (there was nothing to think about) but only to feel her all over my skin, to wonder what had gone wrong, how long it would take to set right. Twenty minutes later the phone rang.

"Hello?" I said, wondering who on earth could be calling now.

"Jean here," said she (a habit she'd picked up on a visit to England two summers before. Jean is a sponge to other people's mannerisms).

"Oh, *Jean!*" said I, pleased.

"I forgot to say goodbye."

"You what?" I said.

"Goodbye," she said distinctly.

And she hung up.

I let a day go by. I didn't do anything because I knew what would happen if I did. It came—I called the co-operative and they said she'd left the day before with all her possessions. Her family didn't know where she was. I said, "You don't *know*?" over the telephone, trying to make them feel as guilty as possible. That's it. This is the painful part. I'm subject to thinking that I've invented things, so for a while the thought kept coming back to me that I'd invented the whole love affair, though that isn't possible, and then the idea that unrequited love is ghastly because it turns into a cult or phantasmagoria, something poisonous, too private a puppet show to exist. I wanted to call the family and tell them I was her wife (or husband) but I didn't think they'd enjoy that. Then I called the co-op again and got the same message—they very obligingly provided me with a second person to talk to, so nobody knew I had called twice. Like calling the weather on the telephone. Nothing but machines left between people. Telephones, taxis, letters, the discarded automata of the modern love affair. I thought perhaps I'd made the whole thing up. This is an awful despair. After the first shock you think, "Well, *that's* over," but what do you do then? The news that kills is the news that makes everything else impossible; you can't sleep or go out or read or watch TV because you can no longer enjoy anything; I had never before realized what a substratum of pure pleasure there is in just going to sleep, for instance. Just eating. All spoiled now.

And I can't tell anyone. I can never tell anyone.

I decided to take a walk, thinking that perhaps I might meet Jean, but I faltered at the bottom of the stairs. Stood for a while on the last step. What a push it takes to get out of the house! Having only imagined it would be—somehow—worse than anything—better to be unhappy—so I forced myself out into a world where everything was lovely (there was a full moon) like a Jean who said "I didn't really mean it, you know" from every black bush, from every gilded housefront. It was a beautiful and horrible sight. I thought of going back to my apartment and writing to Sally and Louise, but they weren't friends. I didn't know them well enough. Besides, what could I ask from them? If I went to visit friends (and I do have other friends) I would have to tell them I'd had a love affair with a man who'd fucked and run; then they'd say, "Oh well, men do that," and I'd say it wasn't like that, we were old friends; so they'd say "Why did he leave?" Because he was a homosexual? Then (they'd say) I was well rid of him and if I kept on grieving I was a fool. There's no equivalent and I can't tell the truth. With each step it got worse, as if I were walking through molasses, my nerves all exposed, what will I do if I meet anyone? (Spies.) So I went back home, hastening all the way. Though I have no home, really. And remembered my past "depressions" when I'd thrown a screen out the window in the powerful, vague fear that otherwise it would be me. All long, long ago, sadly. The rule now is for the wounded to recite, like

Scarlett, oh tomorrow will be another day. I can't get back to my old symbolic craziness. I wished for Count Draculule, but he's dead; all my imaginary monsters are dead. It occurred to me that if Jean had called while I was out, I wouldn't have been able to hear the phone ring, so I ran the last block and up the stairs.

It was quiet. Everything was exactly the same. Everything was just as I had left it: the gleaming refrigerator, the red-and-blue curtains, vinyl table, cupboards, white sink. I thought it would have changed somehow. Oh, the dreariness of that place! I tried to persuade myself that there was still some enjoyment to be got out of it, but it looked dreadful. Nothing there. Nothing elsewhere; my other rooms were equally intolerable. Ditto the outside. People always tell you you'll get over things (and they're right) but what do you do while you're getting over it? The old joke: your wife is buried, you weep on her grave, your friends tell you in a year you'll forget it, you'll go out, meet someone else, get married again. "But what'll I do *tonight?*" I first heard this told about an Italian and it was supposed to show how sex-crazy Italians were (I think), Italian men anyhow, but you know what I mean. In graduate school I'd envied the cats who came into my back yard and rubbed their fat, whiskery faces on the stems of the lilac bush. They had it easy. I lay down on the couch because it hurts less in the horizontal (the old lesson of a seasoned veteran of grief) and I thought I would begin a letter to Sally—no, Louise; Louise looked kinder. But what can you say except "Help me?" They won't fly up here to be my lover. I could be cunning and tell them Mommy and Daddy never loved me. Mummy loved me but she died (weak giggle). I got up to write some sort of letter to them, but realized I hadn't any idea how to begin. Jesus, I didn't want to write anybody. I wanted to feel better is all. Once years and years ago I tried getting drunk when I was miserable; I only became drunk and miserable. What is so astonishing is to realize that not only the people who love you but also husbands and wives, I mean people bound together by a legal tie as real and impersonal as the one that keeps me in classes and pays my salary every month, even these people can just disappear like soap bubbles. And do. But my money will keep coming in every month. That's why money is more reliable than love—people become misers this way. I thought of my work and therefore, grief-drunk, sat down to work; I dusted books and looked through some magazine articles I'd kept to throw away duplicates. I couldn't do anything less routine than that. There's always work to do. Jean called work a blessing.

I sat down at the kitchen table, leaned my face and arms on the cold plastic tablecloth (but it's pretty, it is, it's an unusual deep, pleasant red) and began to weep. No more can I sing: I love my kitchen, my kitchen loves me. There's nothing so awful as being (coming) alive.

They call this mourning, that is: grief work.

George Eliot depicts suffering very well: her heroines just sit in a room and hurt. They don't have the money to do anything else. In lousy novels heroines with broken hearts plunge into "a mad round of dissipation" about which I have only one question, i.e. where do you find it. One academic party A.J. (After Jean) and I was out the door after ten minutes with "a bad headache." You can drive around a lot but a beat-up old station wagon is no Duesenberg (*The Green Hat*, 1920's). Ah! they smoke cigarettes, too, in those books. I called writer friends in Watertown, N.Y., in whose house I've always felt at home, and asked for permission to visit them; I was going to stop over in New York City.

Fine, they said.

My New York friend—only one of them but the one to the purpose, for I wasn't going to see any of those people left over from college, i.e. the amateur Thespian who'd married and moved into the suburbs and who did nothing now but pick up after an immensely destructive two-year-old, or the thirty-year-old insecure spinster who worked for an opera magazine and thought marriage would solve everything, or the Phi Beta Kappa poet who works at a secretarial job, getting drunk on week-ends and wishing she were back at school—as I said, my real, live friend is a gay man a few years older than me. We met after a ballet matinée which I had sat through in such complete, implacable, hostile silence that I had caused several of the people around me to become acutely nervous, at least I certainly hope so. High art doesn't neutralize misery, far from it. And ballet combines obsessively romantic, heterosexual love stories with athletics and you-know-what. (Rose and I after *Swan Lake,* crying into our coffee.) It's ridiculous. I met Stevie at an expensive chain restaurant place on West Eighth that serves nothing but French crèpes; you know, fake wooden beams, fancy Breton costumes on the waitresses, the menu hand-calligraphed in two languages, and right out in the middle of the room (where you could watch the crèpes being made) a large griddle with the fake ménagère of this fake tavern and vats of the stuff they put into their pancakes: spinach, cheese, ham, chestnuts, whipped cream, jam, all that. It's not bad food, really. I was in love with Stevie years and years ago, when I was twenty-one and believed that dreams came true. Thinking of those days—there was my old friend Rose (remember her?), there were splendid pink sunsets in mid-winter when I was coming to group therapy, or summer evenings with the dirty air turning a delicate rose and blue and the trees on Park Avenue (almost dead of the dust) smelling fresh, but only when you were very close to them.

Stevie's a good friend now: willful, tense, hard-working, good to lots of people, extraordinarily well-informed and well-read. He could no more live where I do than a fish could migrate to Death Valley. I saw him before he saw me, and waved; catching sight of me, he patted the place setting opposite him, meaning of course that I should approach and sit down. He beamed at me. He was wearing one of those dreadfully recherché things he loves; this time it was a rhinestone pin in the shape of a pair of kissing lips. Stuck on a fish-net shirt. Which, with leather shorts and sandals, and a Viking beard, gives you some idea why Stevie would be stoned to death in (say) Watertown, N.Y. I sat down and we made nice and kissed each other and exclaimed a lot, and asked about everybody's friends and relations, like the people in *Pooh.* I complimented him on his beard, which had squared off since the last time I'd seen him. I had suddenly and very intensely the feeling that Stevie is smarter than I, braver, stronger, better, more knowing; I admired him and feared him.

I was going to tell him about Jean.

He ordered spinach-and-cheese. I got greedy and ordered chestnuts and whipped cream.

"Well, love, how's the world been treating you?" he said.

I got shy. I described in melodramatic detail the headaches of marking papers, summer cleaning, getting the car fixed, my academic-ugly neighbors.

"Ah, you're a New Yorker at heart," he said.

I told him it wasn't so bad being away if you stayed glued to the TV. We both snickered. I told him my survivor's instincts had become atrophied after such a long time away; I wouldn't be able to function any more. He laughed and shook his head. Then I began hesitantly to tell him that I'd had a bad love affair, using phrases like "the person" or "the other person." It occurred to me that I could even use Jean's real name because people would confuse it with Gene, a man's name.

Finally he said, "Darling Esther, this fellow is *no good*." He had rested his chin in his hands, listening intently.

"He's not a fellow," I said, confused. "He's my best friend."

He tsked and demurred. He smiled and a wry look came into his face. "Would *I* like him?" he said. We'd had a running joke for years about the similarities of our taste in men. I looked down. Red-alerts everywhere. Don't say it; he won't like it. But why not?

"It's a woman," I said.

Stevie said nothing. I guess he's thunderstruck. Surprised, anyway. Despite (or because of) the china collection, his affectation of hating politics, his desire to be a nineteenth-century Russian aristocrat, the rhinestone pins, etc., Stevie is a very good-looking man, and sitting here, trying to cover my embarrassment or my stiffness at his embarrassment or his embarrassment—I feel an eerie return of that love of ten years ago. How I had liked him! (I like him still.) I wanted him because he was unattainable—that was the official version. No. I liked him because he was on my side.

He looked up, his face closed. He said:

"When one gets to a certain age, there's the desire to experiment. You know, to try everything." A year ago I would have agreed.

"No," I said.

Opportunely, the food came.

It was disapproval; it was also a kind of shrinking. Perhaps he wants straight friends. I don't know. When I first met him I was shy, amazed, and very put off, but Stevie doesn't mind middle-class people who are put off; he thrives on it; I've seen him handle roomfuls of middle-class people who disapprove of him and do it so well that everybody went away glowing with conscious virtue. But now I've done something wrong.

We ate silently.

Then he said, rather affected all of a sudden, for Stevie can turn himself inside out like a glove:

"Dear me, this *is* a surprise!"

I began to explain that I had tried to be good but I just couldn't take men any more. Straight men, that is. He said, making a face:

"Oh, I see. Lady's lib."

Now I've asked him before not to call it that. This is Stevie's malicious side: get-away-from-me-or-I'll-scratch. The next step is for me to remember that he's suffered worse than I, that he has been—or could be—beaten up in public, that he could be killed, that nothing I've gone through can hold a candle to what he has. Things always go well after this stage.

"Don't use that word," I said. "It's belittling."

His eyes narrowed. He's going to drawl. He put his chin in his hands, and leaning his elbows on the fake fancy oak of the restaurant table, said deliberately:

"Little Esther's going in for the militant marching and chowder society. You're losing your sense of humor, dear."

I stared.

He said, "You're not gay. You're just being programmatic. For Lady's Lib."

"Women are oppressed," said I suddenly. (What can one say?)

"Oppressed!" cried this sudden stranger in a cracked voice. "You don't know what the word means, darling! Oppression in your happy, sheltered little life?"

He said I was a parasitic, self-indulgent, petty, stupid, bourgeois *woman*.

He said I should try being beaten up by the police.

"Breeders!" he muttered, the color coming back into his face. Breeders is Stevie's term of contempt for the straights.

I told him—but I didn't. I said, "Oh, never mind." The restaurant cuckoo clock struck five. A Bavarian cuckoo clock of carved wood, the wrong thing in the wrong place.

The whole quarrel had taken three and a half minutes.

I left my food—and with wonderful, unconscious cunning, also the check—and hailed a taxi. Leaning my head out the window to refresh myself with the gasoline fumes. Getting my breeder's body sick. I know I can't tell my writer friends about Jean but I'll tell them about feminism because that cuts across everything. When I was seven years old I had a best friend called Yolanda who was Black; I didn't know what being Black meant and I certainly didn't know what being a homosexual meant, but I jolly well knew what being a girl meant. In a then-current Fred Astaire movie called "Yolanda and the Thief" the thief (who was probably Fred Astaire, thinking back on it) danced over the skyline of New York while Yolanda watched him. When Yolanda and I grew up (we planned it that way) we would do the movie over again, only this time it would be Yolanda and me dancing over the tall buildings. Yolanda not only had a wonderful name, she was very independent; she got a quarter from her father every week for mopping the bathroom floor. I tried that but my parents wouldn't let me. They preferred to give me things.

I—the old me who's just got Stevie so mad at her—began to cry in the taxi. It's all such a tiresome puddle of failure. There's this horrible insistence (just as if somebody were riding in the cab next to me and nagging me) that I ought to understand Stevie, that I ought to make allowances, that I've behaved badly, that I'm selfish. I thought of asking the cab-driver to take me to a gay bar, but was interfered with by a memory from a book: woman asks cabbie to take her "where women go." He says "Right, lady," and lets her off at the Y.W.C.A. Years ago a painter friend of mine was stopped on Eighth Street by a small, dark foreign man with a monobrow who hissed at him from behind one hand, "Where are the secret places?" My friend, of course, did not know. As he said:

If you can't make it with the people you know—
   Then what?
Anyway it's got nothing to do with me; I'm not a Lesbian.
Lesbians. Lez-bee-yuns. Les beans. Les human-beans?
   I'm a Jean-ist.
A nasty little tune I couldn't place followed me into the cab,
to my hotel, through the Metropolitan Museum the next day,
out to the airport, like a snail leaving disgusting little tracks on
the European paintings, the Middle Eastern carpets, the fancy
airport luncheon, the jets taking off, everything I am supposed to enjoy. It was about somebody looking for a job in the
last century and never getting one because (here the refrain
would come in):

> I asked the reason why.
> He said, Now don't you see that sign?
> *No Irish need apply.*

   Though it was about a man looking for a job, not a woman.
Always a man.

   Pain is boring. That's the worst of it. I cried so much in those
two days that I had to put on dark glasses in self-defense. I
won't bother you with the details: the sobbing in the public
rest room, the haughty, injured look you put on to conceal the
fact that you've been crying. I flew up to—sounds very sophis-
ticated, doesn't it?—but my plane was a tiny one of a line I
won't mention, a sort of flying Toonerville Trolley that carries
baby chicks and live lobsters as often as people (and airmail)
and sits out on the field as if in flat denial of the laws of
aerodynamics: You mean I'm going to fly in *that*? Half the
stops are made in ports that don't have central towers or
ground-to-air radio; you just come in for a good look and take
the chance that nobody else wants to land on the same patch of
grass. I found myself next to a little old Italian lady who was
carrying vast quantities of bundles: bread, salami, cheese,
wool, sausages, sweaters, God knows what. It seems this was
stuff her relatives had given her. She explained in bad English
that she'd come in on the morning plane and was going back
on the afternoon one. We spread her bundles on the seats

behind us (Toonerville is never full) and then I hid behind a
book. The affront of all that upstate New York scenery—blue
sky, white clouds, mountain-colored mountains (as the Chinese say). Promises, promises. A young unmarried couple (no
ring) across the aisle was reading a copy of *Life* magazine, sort
of leafing through it and looking at the pictures. They were
working-class Appalachia, I suspect, covering bad nutrition
and lack of means with lots of make-up in her case and lots of
self-assertiveness in his. She wore a beehive hairdo and
sneakers with her pink dress, he, some sort of sleazy, green
rayon suit. She looked around the plane slowly and won-
deringly (it was almost empty except for us and a family in
back), apparently rather bored, and said:
"I bet this next election will be different because—" (here
she named a current government scandal).
"No it won't," he said. "Why should it? It won't be. That's
full of crap." And he went back to reading. She looked around
again, a little desperately—it's not boredom, just the last-
ditch, lip-wetting, oh what shall I do now. They leafed
through the pictures.
"Oh hey," she said, "look at that. Isn't that weird? It says
we're all descended from fish. Just imagine, a million years
ago your great-great-great-grandaddy was a fish." I thought
this rather imaginative. He twitched the magazine page out of
her fingers, saying sharply:
"Jesus, you'd believe anything."
Again the glance round, to hide her embarrassment. She
was radiating dumbness in all directions. We all know that
self-deprecating uh-oh I put my foot in it. She got stupider
and prettier as I watched (from behind my book). Finally she
wet her lips and with an exaggeratedly casual air, slipped her
arm under his and made a little kissing face at him. This he
liked. So they began to neck. Imagine forty years of this.
Think how girls like that idealize men who "act like gentle-
men." I attempted to disappear into my seat and meditated
why beautiful always means expensive, why in order to be
"naturally beautiful" you need the clever haircut, the skin
conditioner, the good diet, the cod liver oil, the dental work,
the fashionably-fitting clothes, the expensive shampoo, the

medical bills, the exercise. Always money. The voices of my inarticulate, radical young students are full of money.

Then I thought of Jean, who radiates not only money but a frightening personal force, a truly terrifying, unconsicous determination—she thinks everybody has it. I drifted away, pleased at first, then remembered she didn't want me. Bad.

I was rescued by a thunderstorm, water shivering across the windows and blue glare you wouldn't believe. The plane dropped twenty feet and left our stomachs on the ceiling. The pilot (chuckling on the intercom) told us he'd gotten careless heh heh, and it was only a little local storm heh heh and we'd be out of it in a minute and into Watertown. Wow, a joke, right?

It got better but not much; there was a bad, bumpy descent and I began to get airsick.

The pilot is amused. Someone has placed that abominable young couple right in my way when we all know such scenes of mutual neurosis and degradation are few and far between in this our free, modern, sexually liberated land.

Is somebody trying to tell me something?

Hugh and Ellen Selby live in Watertown, N.Y., near the Canadian border, in a vast, rambling Charles Addams mansion—there is a story that a leak in the roof once had to be repaired by helicopter. Their place has been a mecca for their friends for years. The Selbys, because they are writers, know what nobody else does: I mean, why writers need quiet, why they keep odd hours, why people can't always stay where they're born, why publishers are no good at all, why sitting still and thinking is hard work. He edits various kinds of specialized technical books; she writes children's fantasies, very good ones. Ellen grew up in Kansas, in some Fundamentalist sect (which I never got quite straight)—no cards, no dancing, no movies, no make-up, no drinking. She takes children and what children read very seriously. Hugh comes from a more ordinary small town but when asked about it he will only giggle and light wooden matches with his feet (honest); but I understand that they both left their respective homes as soon as they could. Ellen is the steady one; Hugh is short, fat, and wears old-fashioned striped bathing suits in the summer, over which his uncut grey beard floats like Spanish moss. The Selbys, in addition to planting the delphiniums in their front yard in a hammer-and-sickle pattern, have inside their house a vast portrait of Grandfather Mao—this is a joke but the neighbors can't be trusted to understand it.

Ellen cooks—plainly but well. Hugh has water-fights and greenpea-fights in restaurants (sometimes).

There are in the Selby mansion four fireplaces, a tank of tropical fish, statuettes of monsters from outer space, a living room thirty feet by thirty feet, and a miscellaneous collection of Victorian plush furniture: green and rose-red are the predominant colors.

Some of the furniture is falling apart.

You find manuscripts everywhere, sometimes even in the (separate) garage.

My friends' one fault is that they don't believe names run in cycles and that the name of their infant daughter—Anya—is part of the new wave of fashion after Sherri, Debbi, Dee, and Leslie. Little Ivan, little Anya, little Tobias, are the names of the future. The Selbys think they picked out their daughter's name all by themselves.

Aside from that, it's the best of all possible worlds.

I took a taxi from the airport and walked in; Ellen was in the kitchen. When she heard me, she came out and put her arms around me.

"Mm," I said. "What do I smell?" (Something cooking, that is.) My insides know that the Selbys are my real momma and poppa. They themselves often mention young writers who want to be adopted by them, but I've never presumed so far. I went out at Ellen's direction into the back yard to get lettuce from the kitchen garden. I'm such a bad cook—or rather a non-cook (I often get interested in reading and let the food burn) that I eat well only when at friends' houses. Years ago I used to be very embarrassed at the awkwardness of my first hour with the Selbys, each time I visited—I used to think it was my fault—but now we all seem to accept it. It's one of those things that happens with friends one sees only twice a year.

I gave Ellen the lettuce to wash—she insists she knows where everything is and I'd only be in the way—and watched while she chopped it into the salad. Ellen is forty-five and trim rather than pretty; nonetheless her gestures and attitudes have that extraordinary interest or glamor or beauty or what-have-you that some people radiate. One might call it authority or one might call it love. I don't mean that I love Ellen in the ordinary way or that I'm sexually attracted to her. I mean she's a blessing.

Hugh is a mad, plump owl (his round glasses) who hangs from ceilings, wiggling his bare toes. (He has actually been known to do this when parties occur in houses with exposed beams.)

Ellen took clothes out of the washer and put them in the dryer. She let me help her set the dinner table in the next room: i.e. she handed me the dishes and I took them in. The Selbys have a dinner table that seats fourteen, though there are seldom that many people in the house at one time.

"No, four," said Ellen.

"Anya?" I said. (Anya is two months old.)

"Somebody else," she said. She went down into the cellar for canned goods and preserves. (She puts up preserves, too.)

Just before dinner Hugh descended from the higher regions of the house, glasses and all, and started poking into the oven (after saying hello to me, of course). Letters and packages were scattered all over the kitchen; he started opening some of them and making interested noises: chuckles, mimed disbelief, sounds of wonder. I took paper napkins into the dining room and laid them in a heap on the table. (The Selbys are not formal.) We trooped into the dining room, where Ellen had laid out everything on those heat-proof pads.

The bell rang.

"There she is," said Ellen. She and Hugh looked guardedly at each other; they had apparently been trapped into having dinner with someone they didn't like. We don't want that one here. I saw "that one" in the old pier glass opposite the coat rack in the hall—a series of blue-and-white reflections spotted and stained by the leprosy of the old glass—and then I saw her come in through the kitchen.

"Leslie," said Ellen. "this is Esther."

"Esther, Leslie," said Hugh, satisfied.

Leslie was a tall twenty-two-year-old with long fair hair like Alice Liddell's, long legs in impeccable, flared white trousers, white wedgies, and a blue, clinging, frilly nylon tank top that kept pulling up above her belly-button. I had never seen such expensive clothes. She was an ex-student from Richmond, Va. who "wrote" and who had come to Watertown only God knows why; she had taken a small house outside of town, she said. As she ate her salad, she kept pulling languidly at the tank top to get it to meet her trousers, but you could see that this was only a gesture; her heart wasn't in it.

Ellen helped her to some canned paté.

"Merci," said Leslie, with an impeccable accent. I had a sudden yen to announce that I could understand only Yiddish. Leslie talked for a while about her family's maid in Richmond and how the maid was phobic about snakes in the garden but had to go there every day to get flowers for the dinner table.

They had a wonderful dog named Champion, a malemute who had to stay indoors in the air-conditioning most of the year. Leslie went right on, all about Mother and Father and the maid and the cook. She thought her own girlhood was fascinating.

Leslie had been the most beautiful girl in Richmond.

Ellen was getting annoyed at being addressed in snippets of French, I could tell. The way she shows it is that she gets very steady, very controlled, and her voice becomes perfectly civil.

Leslie said, "Georgie and I think we'll go to Greece this fall. When I go back home in September, I'll just have to leave, you know. I couldn't stand the winter." She started talking about this island they'd gone to the year before which nobody else had discovered yet; you had to get there by water-taxi. Georgie (she explained) was Georgette, the teacher Leslie had been living with ever since she'd graduated from the University of South Florida. Georgie had an awful lot of money. But the owner of the apartment building where she and Georgie lived in Richmond wouldn't let them take Titi to the swimming pool on the roof. Wasn't that awful? Titi was a silver Siamese with marvelous blue eyes. Their building had a swimming pool, a boutique, a doorman, a sauna, a private TV system, and a quartz solarium. Their apartment had eight rooms. Leslie started to talk about a science fiction story she was going to write (about "a girl of the future") but at this point Ellen remembered something she had to go get in the kitchen. (Or the attic or the cellar). I excused myself and followed her. Ellen, of course, was not looking for anything but simply standing over the kitchen table and trying to control her temper.

"That—that *girl* never writes anything!" said Ellen.

"Look on the bright side," I said. "If she did, you'd have to read it."

"They live in two rooms," said Ellen vehemently, "she and that—that teacher of hers." (Georgie, it turned out, was a solid, middle-aged former Bostonian who had maddened Ellen by coming up once to visit her protegée and lecturing the Selbys about literature for two and one half hours by the clock. I assumed it was the usual collision of bad academic with real writer.)

"Do you think they're—" I said, embarrassed.

"I don't care," said Ellen. "I don't want to know. It's bad enough as it is." I remembered another young writer friend (male) who had come into Ellen's kitchen three winters before, having returned from his first European tour, and said, "Ellen, darling, I've found out the most astonishing thing about myself," while both Ellen and Hugh listened with weary patience, everybody else but the young writer having guessed it all long ago.

They don't really understand, of course.

We went back to the dining room and finished dinner— plain, fine food. Leslie didn't eat much; she never ate much. After the cherry pie she jumped up (did she know what we wanted of her?) and said she had to go, she'd almost forgotten, she was so sorry but she had to meet somebody who had a motorcycle. He was going to take her some place for a drink. I regarded Alice Liddell's pretty Anglo-Saxon face, her marvelous blue eyes, and foresaw the day when she'd burst into tears in the Selby's living room, begging them, "How can I change!"

She went out, and three carefully-scheduled minutes later Hugh whooped. (Out of hearing, I suppose.) He told me that when they'd first met, she'd asked him his name and he'd said, "Just call me Hugh," whereupon she'd said, bewildered, "But what's your name?" He fluffed his beard with his fingers like actors in Chinese opera do to indicate rage. He blew into it, too.

We took our coffee into the living room, in front of the empty fireplace (summer nights near the Canadian border can be cold) and Ellen began to talk about the current ruin of the world in general and New York State in particular. Since the last time I'd seen her she'd become passionately involved in ecology—not the organic foods kind, the all-over kind. I know that bitter, hopeless desperation—the petitions, the radio appeals, the placards, the letter campaigns, the demonstrations. It's like trying to move a locomotive with your bare hands. Hugh nodded amiably and vanished upstairs to edit something; I yelled after him, "But Hugh—what does an editor *do*?" He chuckled. Ellen talked, hunched over, her hands trembling with continual anger; swamps were being drained all over the country, forests were being covered with asphalt, fish and algae were being killed. I said, "I know how you feel. There's something—"

"Tomorrow," I said. "I'll tell you tomorrow."

The Selbys guest room is on their third floor, with a tiny mirror tacked to one wall, an old farm sink (iron) from which you can get cold water only, and the real bathroom a long flight of stairs down. I took a good look at my face in the bathroom mirror that night because I knew I wouldn't get to see it again until morning (would it change? I wonder!). I have a melancholy Jewish face, big-featured, lean, and hungry. A prophet's face. In some novel somewhere there's a Jewish character, a big fat man who fled Germany in the late 30's and who says Why travel? Wait, and they'll chase you around the world.

I kept the subject successfully at bay for most of the next

day. Hugh and Ellen worked in the afternoon, so after browsing in their library, I walked into town to visit the local florist (who sold mostly garden plants—tomatoes, started green peppers, that sort of thing) and then on to the five-and-ten, browsing through the drugstore magazines, having a soda, and so on. There aren't many possibilities in Watertown. I had lunch in a hamburger place (gummy cottage cheese, tired fruit) and walked back to the Selbys', scuffing my feet in the dust at the side of the highway, watching the white Queen Anne's Lace which blossoms everywhere at this time of year. Wild carrot.

I knew I would have to tell Ellen. Otherwise why be friends? I mean if it's not to be unreal.

There was another guest for dinner.

For a moment I thought it might be Leslie's friend who'd taken her out the night before—there was a motorcycle outside the house—but anyway inside it there was a friend of the Selbys called Carl, and I will call him Carl Muchomacho. This may be unfair. I remembered a satire he'd written in which there was (presented with unique completeness) the fantasy woman of a certain kind of freak male: I mean the sexy, earthy chick who loves motorcycles (because she has orgasms on them), who makes pottery, who balls all the time, who isn't uptight about anything, and who never gets pregnant. So Muchomacho is a satirical name. Carl has an attractive swagger, a pleasant, lean face, a dark moustache, and what is called a sense of humor.

But I wasn't in the right mood.

When I came in he got to his feet (he'd been having a drink with Hugh) and—with a flourish—offered me one of the old, plushy, green, Victorian chairs. They're hard things to push across a rug, by which I gather that Muchomacho was turning his sense of humor against himself. I said:

"Oooh, thanks, but I didn't know you were into that sort of thing."

"What sort of thing?" said he.

"Gallantry," I said.

"Well, I hope you were pleasantly surprised," says Carl, rocking back and forth a little on the balls of his feet. He's one of those restless, springy types who can never stand still.

"Surprised, anyway," I said. He smiled. The conversation is picking up. Here is a witty lady with whom he can fence. He said, "You don't dig it?"

"Well, no, not really," I said.

"Why not?"

"Oh, never mind," I said. "It's not worth—I don't want to talk about it all *this* much!" And I laughed. Hugh and Ellen exchanged happy glances of marital complicity: See-it's-working-out-I-told-you-she'd-like-him.

"But why not?" said Muchomacho, sincerely interested.

"It's not important," I said, so he supplied what my modesty would not or could not; he said:

"You mean you don't want to be a lady?" (smiling)

"That's right," I said. He looked interested and expectant. I squashed the suspicion that he and the Selbys were putting me on. I really don't think so.

"Well then," said Carl logically, "how *do* you want to be treated? Would you rather I ignored you? Or pulled the chair out from under you?" Hugh chuckled. Witty Hugh.

"Don't be silly," I said, controlling myself and trying not to sound like a governess; "Just treat me—well, decently. Like anyone."

"Like Hugh?" said clever Muchomacho. ("Please!" exclaimed Hugh happily.) Ellen looked as calm as if nothing were happening. I said, a little sharply:

"I'll tell you, the one thing I do not want to do is continue this discussion all through dinner." This time Ellen looked up.

"Sorry, but I didn't start it," said Carl pleasantly.

I got up, excused myself with a smile, and went to the bathroom. I figured that five minutes later they'd be talking about something else and so they were; then I got sneaky and introduced the topic of food additives so we had ecology all through dinner. Everybody listened respectfully. Carl, I am quite sure, did not care for the topic, but he honored it. After dessert we all moved back into the living room while Hugh started a fire in the fireplace; then Carl Muchomacho came over and stood at the back of my chair, saying lightly:

"At the risk of incurring your savage, feminist wrath, can I ask you out with me tonight?"

"Huh?" I said (and jumped).

"Can I take you out and show you a good time?" he said, adding, "I'm really harmless, you know."

"Oh, thanks," I said, "but—" (trailed off, trying to think of an excuse. I just washed my hair?)

"Frankly, I feel rotten," I said. I don't want to go anywhere or do anything; I just want to sit."

"You can sit on my motorcycle," he said.

"I don't feel up to it," I said.

"Come on," he said, "It'll do you good. Get a little wind in your hair." The Selbys glanced at each other again. They too seemed to think it would do me good. I shook my head. Carl shrugged. We did not go on to have one of those endless arguments about whether sitting on a motorcycle is the same thing as sitting at home and when I said I didn't want to do anything, what did I mean by "do" and what does "mean" mean. Perhaps he's just getting too old to be persistent. He turned to Hugh, saying "See? I do treat you two alike," and proposed they go out somewhere to have a beer.

Which they did. (Though he didn't promise to show Hugh a good time.) Ellen said nothing but she looked at me disapprovingly.

I said, "Ellen, I just can't face it. Not again." (Which was only a small lie.) Then I burst into tears. They were unsynmpathetic, angry tears and they didn't get me any approval.

I can't tell her.

She said dryly that Carl was a good friend of theirs.

I said wasn't I?

She said softly and exasperatedly, "Oh, Esther!"

"Never mind," I said; "I'll call him tomorrow." (That's what dating's all about; it's to please your Mother. Darling, he looked like such a nice boy. But he's impotent, Mother.)

"You've changed," said Ellen gravely.

I said that yes, I had; I'd gotten a lot into feminism since I'd seen her last. Ellen knows better than to believe in bra-burners; she thought for a minute and then said carefully, "I suppose I've always been a feminist. You know, where I grew up it was impossible for a woman to have a career at all; she could only be a wife and mother, but here I am with both."

I said Yes, wasn't that wonderful.

She smiled.

"And Hugh does half the housework," I said, "and takes care of the baby." (Anya was at the baby-sitter's because I was there.) "Ah! that's unusual."

"He helps," said Ellen. Then she said, "I don't mind doing it." They all start out by assuming you mean somebody else: third-world women, welfare mothers, Fundamentalist Baptists, Martians. We went through all that. I told her that I meant us both, that I wouldn't have my job at all if I hadn't been twice as good as my colleagues.

"Make the world safe for mediocrity," I said.

She said she didn't care to know mediocre people and she certainly hoped I didn't.

I said, "That's not the point." (But I didn't know what was the point, not then.) I said, "Ellen, when you were with your first husband, when you were trying to write and had two children, wouldn't day care have helped? You couldn't have afforded a baby sitter then. And wouldn't it have helped if your family and the clergyman and all those people hadn't tried to shove you right back into your old place? I mean if they thought it was O.K.? My God, you lost your voice for two years."

"That's Fundamentalism," she said.

"Oh no it's not," I said, "look at TV, look at the magazines, look how convenient it is to have a wife, look at the ads."

"Esther, no one I respect believes what they see on TV or in the ads! For goodness' sakes, neither do you."

I said ha ha the things we took least seriously might affect us the most (T.S. Eliot). Clincher.

"Besides," I added, "you told me once you had to get up at 5 A.M. for four years to write because there wasn't any other time."

"If one wants something, one makes sacrifices," said she.

I asked if Hugh had made sacrifices.

"We are different people," said Ellen.

She added, "He may have made other kinds of sacrifices. I'm not going to defend him to you, Esther. The point is that we have to make our individual choices and lead our lives, man or woman, and everybody suffers one way or another. Life is compromise. And that's something none of us can evade. Whether man or woman."

I said furiously that I'd had quite enough of all this literary book club tragic-sense-of-life as an excuse for other people's privileges.

"You're bitter!" said she.

"Sure," I said. "Malcolm no-name saw his daddy killed before his eyes at the age of four and that's political; but I see my mother making a dish-rag of herself every day for thirty years and that's personal."

Ellen said my mother was responsible for that, if it was true, and we didn't have to repeat our mother's mistakes.

I said didn't we just!

She said, "I've seen you over-reacting to all sorts of trivial, harmless things. If your ideas—"

"It's not trivial or harmless. It happens too often. It's just part of the whole damn thing. And don't tell me he didn't do anything that bad, I know he didn't, but the code of manners is only a symptom of the whole damn thing."

A long silence.

"As far as I can see," said Ellen steadily, "you want people to treat you according to some strange and special code of behavior that only you understand. That's hardly rational, Esther." She was looking down at her hands. As far as Ellen is concerned, this whole subject is finshed because Ellen is Superwoman; if Ellen's responsible for everything, that's because it's her choice; Ellen still exists on five hours' sleep a night. I said nothing of this, only that I wasn't alone in my beliefs. I wasn't a Saucerian or an occultism nut, and I guessed it was the old argument about the cup being half empty or half full. We'd never settle it. Anyway, George Bernard Shaw said there is no great art without some fanaticism behind it, so I was starting ahead of the game, right? Her, too. Look at her and ecology.

Ellen said very quietly and distinctly, "I am not a fanatic."

I said, "No, no, I don't *mean* that." But she said again: "I am not a fanatic."

"Oh well, all fanaticism means," (said I) "is a truth some-body else won't accept. So we're both fanatics."

Ellen's anger only makes her more controlled. She changed the subject. Far be it from me to suppose she picks her beliefs for their acceptability to her husband's friends. She told me about a mutual acquaintance of ours who had become—God save us!—a Satanist and had sacrificed goats in the back of occult bookstores.

"Where on earth did he get the goats?" I said.

Ellen said it wasn't funny; he'd ended up in a mental hospital.

"You meet the best people there," I said.

"Esther, he's in a *mental hospital*." Not understanding my lack of understanding of her understanding of my under-standing. I said I was sorry; I hadn't meant to be flip.

"Look, Ellen," I said, "I feel as if I'd been flayed, I mean I'm all nerves. I never should've come. I'll go tomorrow and call back in a few months. When I'm human again."

She said, looking right at me, "If this new belief of yours has such a bad effect on your relations with others, I think you ought to re-examine your belief."

(Years ago, when I was in group therapy, I wore "Bohe-mian" clothes: cheap Indian-print shifts, cheap Mexican dresses, lots of color, big old copper jewelry. This was long before such things became fashionable. The group didn't like the way I dressed; they said I only did it to get attention. They said, "You're trying to be different." This was also the stan-dard explanation for juvenile delinquency that year. I said I dressed that way because I liked it and not because I wanted attention, because I did get gawked at and teased in the street, and that I definitely did not enjoy.

(They smiled.

(They said Oh, so you don't like looking different?

(I said I didn't like being teased.

(*Then why,* said they triumphantly, *do you dress the way you do?*)

I said good-night and went upstairs. My friend Ellen with her endless work and her earnest assurances to an interviewer last year that *her* children always took preference over her work in emergencies (Hugh is a hit-and-run father) and that she hoped more and more women would experience the fulfillment of both work and motherhood. "No one must go beyond me," she said. Do you know the last time the percentage of women in the professions and women Ph.D.'s and women entering colleges was as high as it is today?

In nineteen-twenty, that's when.

And you'd think friends—but Carl is her friend; the truth is that she prefers Carl to me.

There's this club, you see. But they won't let you in. So you cry in a corner for the rest of your life or you change your ways and feel rotten because it isn't you, or you go looking for another club. But this club is the world. There's only one.

"Why do you people go where you're not wanted?"

"Why do *you* go where you're not wanted? *I* don't want you." (My maternal uncle, at a resort that didn't like Jews.)

If Jean had stayed with me I wouldn't have cared, but now I must put on my putrid ankle sox and my cheerleader button because there's no right of private judgment and you can't think of yourself; you have to be thought. By others. Why did Ellen forget the classic exchange? I mean the one where they say But aren't you for human liberation? and you say Women's liberation is for women, not men, and they say You're selfish. First you have to liberate the children (because they're the future) and then you have to liberate the men (because they've been so deformed by the system) and then if there's any liberation left you can take it into the kitchen and eat it.

Oh, I must be bad. I'm hostile. I'm bitter. I'm hideously wicked. I must be crazy or I wouldn't suffer so. Taking things personally—! (Persons shouldn't take things personally.) I stood in my traveling pajamas over the iron sink, brushing my teeth and crying—how could she, how *could* she!—and when I straightened up, somebody else looked out at me from the tiny mirror tacked to the wall.

Who is that marvelous woman!

I was so pleased, she's so cute, with toothpaste around her mouth like a five-year-old. I like her, really. She's Esther who loves everything systematic and neat but it's all moonshine;

she has elaborate schemes for traveling with a traveling iron
and a collapsible miniature ironing board (which is too heavy
to carry), and a traveling sewing case (which is *very* small), and
traveling clothes which don't need ironing (so why take the
iron!), and shoe-trees made of plastic so they'll be light, and a
collapsible toothbrush with a marvelous plastic case, and airmail stamps which she never uses.

Wonderful, silly Esther.

So my reflection comforted me and blew me stars and
kisses. I thought of Jean—who'd left me—and Ellen—who
hated me—and my own crazy nastiness, which is that I don't
like men and I'm giving up on them and I don't care about
them so I'm a monster and God will strike me dead. Sleeping
with women is all right if it's just play, but you must never let it
interfere with your real work, which is sleeping with men.

The mirror didn't believe it.

So I slipped into triumph in spite of everything, like an
Eskimo lady in a nine-days' blizzard on an ice-floe. And very
humble (but giggling) I went to bed.

I pray that She my soul may keep. (snf)

Thinking how nice it was to be horizontal when you're tired,
and that after a non-committal, guilty, bland breakfast with the
Selbys, after my rather lame excuses about catching a virus or
not feeling well or something, after Hugh drives me to the
airport and they say "Goodbye" and I say "Goodbye" and after
I write a very nasty letter to my New York glamorous media
friends who think bisexuality is groovy (but only for women
and only if you're married and only if you like men better)
there is something else I must do, an option Ellen didn't think
of.

What do you do when the club won't let you in, when there's
no other, and when you won't (or can't) change? Simple.

You blow the club up.

(The mystery of courage. The mystery of enjoyment. One
moves incurably into the future but there is no future; it has to
be created. So it all ends up totally unsupported, self-caused,
that symbol of eternity, The Snake Biting Its Own Tail. I'm
strong because I have a future; I have a future because I willed
it; I willed it because I'm strong. Unsupported.

(Ezekial saw the wheel
(Way up in the middle of the air—
(O Ezekial saw the wheel
(Way in the middle of the air!

(Now the big wheel runs by faith
(And the little wheel runs by the grace of God—

(The above made up by professional hope experts, you might say, because willful, voluntary, intentional hope was the only kind they had in anything like long supply. Faith is not, contrary to the usual ideas, something that turns out to be right or wrong, like a gambler's bet; it's an act, an intention, a project, something that makes you, in leaping into the future, go so far, far, far ahead that you shoot clean out of Time and right into Eternity, which is not the end of time or a whole lot of time or unending time, but timelessness, that old Eternal Now. So that you end up living not in the future (in your intentional "act of faith") but in the present. After all.

(Courage is *willful* hope.)

Summer is dying. The airfield's still rank with Queen Anne's lace—its flowers look like white parasols—but the goldenrod's coming out too, and even a few blue asters, which means the beginning of the end. On a sunny afternoon you know summer will last forever, all that iridescent blue and green, but the nights are colder now. Three hours after sunset you can smell autumn. The pilot came in by sight after circling our cow pasture (we don't have ground-to-air communication here either) and I walked to my battered old heap in the parking lot. Home along the roads I know so well: butter-and-eggs (that's like tiny, yellow-and-white snapdragons), purple chicory, which I've heard called corn flowers or flax flowers, and the very few last (battered but game) black-eyed Susans. Everything was growing up through the hay like hair. We'll have hot weather again before October. I went through the town and up the hill, parking in my old place at the top, which is so awful to get into in winter because of the ice, and then hauled my suitcase upstairs, picking up on the way a note my landlady had slipped under my door. I forgot to pay the rent before I left. I opened the windows, disconnected the timer from the living-room lamp, ran water in both sinks until the faucets stopped spitting at me, all the things you have to do when you come back. You know. I was putting clothes away with one hand (mostly the laundry bag which hangs on the inside of the bedroom closet) and carrying the note in the other, with that unaccountable, feverish efficiency that comes over me whenever I come home and have to get everything put away and fixed up again. My suitcase gaped open on the bed and I kept having to step over a pair of shoes. The note said:

"...how you buy a gun. You giggle a lot and tell the clerk your boy friend wants you to go hunting with him so you have to get a hunting rifle. You say Oh gee he told me to ask *you;* he said you'd know—"

I started again:

"Dearest Esther,

"Now I'm in town and you're not. I'm at 14 Tighe Street, number in the book under Anderson. Sorry I got scared and ran away. I went to Boston, to some friends, and learned a lot. Then I came back and just messed around. Do you remember three years ago, after the bomb scare, the University was going to keep lists of students who took suspicious books out of the University library? But the best bomb handbook turned out to be the Encyclopedia Britannica.

"This is how you buy a gun. You giggle a lot and tell the clerk your boy friend wants you to go hunting with him so you have to get a hunting rifle. You say Oh gee he told me to ask *you;* he said you'd know everything. Then you keep your ears open. You'll pay too much the first time but that's O.K. Don't try to pretend you had it all written down on a piece of paper but lost it; they'll only send you out to get your instructions again. I know. And remember: *you're only a girl.*

"As soon as your lights stop going on and off so regularly, I'll know you're back. I'll call or you call me; I want to talk to you.

Love,
Jean."

"P.S. I hope you're not mad at me.

"P.P.S. I keep Brown Bess in her wrappings in the kitchen. I can take her apart, clean her, put her back together again, load and unload her, and pot a tin can at fifty feet. When nobody's around I talk to her because I love her. I call her Blunderbess.

"P.P.P.S. I love you, too."

I re-read Jean's letter. I read it until it didn't make sense any more. I brewed myself a cup of tea, then threw the tea in the sink. I don't want to go through that again, whether she loves me or doesn't love me, whatever "love" means. It's all spoilt. When I was very young—I mean eighteen years ago—I fell in love with a man who didn't know how to drive a car properly; when we hit a patch of ice on the roadway once, he steered against the skid and we went half-way across the road in a sort of figure-eight; he told me complacently that this was the right thing to do and I knew it wasn't but I didn't care because I adored him. Twenty-five years ago we had parties to which the boys didn't come, or if they did they wouldn't dance or talk or do anything. Twenty years ago I went to college and began to recognize that I was invisible; having dressed for a date (dates were absolutely crucial then) in my low heels, my nylons, my garter belt, my horsehair petticoat, my cotton petticoat, my taffeta skirt, my knit jersey blouse, my circle pin, my gold earrings, my charm bracelet, my waist-cincher, my lipstick, my little bit of eye-shadow, my heavy faille coat, my nail polish, my mohair scarf, and my gloves, I went into the dormitory garden to wait for him. The garden was full of late spring flowers. I had already admired myself in the full-length mirror on the back of my closet door—and that was very nice indeed, proving that I could look good—but standing between the stone walls on the stone-flagged walk, watching the flowers grow ever lighter and more disembodied in the blue twilight—and sitting on the stone bench under the Gothic arches and all that ivy—and we were supposed to get A's and use the library—we were supposed to write papers—we were supposed to be *scholars*—I wanted to take off all my clothes and step out of my underwear. And then take off my hair and fingernails and my face and my flesh and finally my very bones. Just to step out of it. All the way out of it.

My date said, "There you are!"

If I was dying, my mother'd give me a cup of tea. So many times we've sat in the kitchen and fiddled with the tea things and talked inconsequential nonsense; then Daddy came home and admired us both, carefully urging Mother not to be so afraid of so many things, and Mother said she felt better and would go put on something nice.

But never did. Out of some furious, sullen instinct, she never did. She'd always ruin the effect somehow. And about most middle-aged women, don't they always ruin the effect somehow—too childish, too drab, too careful, too flamboyant, too frumpish, too expensive, too something? A genuine Picasso on which someone has scrawled at the bottom, "This is a fake"—or even more cleverly, "This is *not* a fake!"—so of course it's a double fake.

Did I tell you that my mother was the child of immigrant parents and that she taught herself to read English before she went to school? She never worked (I mean outside the house) so she had lots of time to make up fairy tales for me. They always began, "There was a little girl who—" I was immensely flattered. In her middle age she got fat, as if on purpose, gave up reading anything but historical novels because she said she couldn't understand what was written nowadays ("my poor brain"). She died at seventy, keeping to the end her invincible stupidity and her defiant, uncanny, extraordinarily thorough bad taste. That woman could make a shroud look tacky. I wish she'd come back and show me so we could have a good talk about it.

My father, about whom I'm sure you've been wondering, was a nice, ordinary man who did not have that intuitive understanding of feminine psychology always attributed to nice men in novels written by nice women for nice women. He didn't believe in the pretty, mindless muffin who's the style now—that wasn't in his time and it would have offended his sense of propriety anyway—nor did he believe in the busty roll-in-the-hay type (which was the thing in my teens)—to tell you the truth, I don't know what type of woman he did believe in. He used to read Sunday newspaper editorials about science (he thought of himself as an Informed Layman) although he tended to enjoy the physics most and to be skeptical about psychology. He praised and encouraged my mother, rather (I'm afraid) on the assumption that she was a kind of invalid, trying to cure her of her phobias, her daydreams, her distaste for people at parties, her insistence that she was stupid, her sleeping eleven hours a night, her love of gardens, her fairytales, her disbelief in science, her inability to learn to drive a car. He once remarked to me that he'd married her because she was "different"—then I suppose he had to change her back again. Or maybe he got more difference than he'd bargained for. I don't know. It's hard to tell what he thought of women because he always spoke of us with great formal deference.

"What Man can conceive, Man can achieve!" my father would exclaim, looking up from his Sunday-supplement article or his book of popular science.

My mother once confided in me that she didn't believe in atoms. I asked her what the world was made of, then. She thought for a minute.

"Elves," she said.

If she came back into my kitchen now, severely silly, dumpy and deliberately dowdy in her grave-clothes, how could I explain to her that it wasn't all her fault, after all? What could I say to her?

"Mama, how good it is to see you! What's it like being dead? Never mind, I know. Come have a cup of tea." We putter about. I put on the kettle. I gossip and chatter a little. I apologize for going over to Daddy's side when I was in my teens; after all, what else could I do? I was terrified he would think of me as he thought of her. Besides, the world isn't made of elves, not really. She cries a little. Then she shrugs. I say, "Mama, I'm going to tell you a fairy tale.

"It's about a middle-aged scientist who was also a politician and an army officer and a revolutionary and a judge and in Congress and a genius mathematician and a poet. And she—"

Why bother, why bother. I want the matriarchy. I want it so badly I can taste it. I *should* put a rug on the bedroom floor (which is all bare wood); I *shouldn't* have these thoughts.

There's an actor on the Late Late Show I'm in love with—is that going to be my love life for the next thirty years, watching 1:30 A.M. TV? Suppose he wears out. Suppose I don't like him any more. Suppose they show other things. O idiocy! "Sorry I got scared and ran away." So you pick yourself up as if nothing had happened. Easy to say!

I don't want her.

I went about my business for the next two days, and if you're wondering about what I'm going to feel when Jean turns up, well so am I.

I spent my time in the library, picking out obscure references to memoirs written by bad ladies two hundred years ago and novels by worse ladies who, though personally blameless, wrote bad books. *A Romance of the Pyrenees, Marianna, or The Puritan's Daughter.* Weird, icky stuff. I've lost my awe of the library completely: this vast, defunct megalith over which we little mammals wander, nipping and chewing bits of its skin. I rip away at a little pocket: some authoress who wrote five romances (five!) under the pseudonym *By A Lady.* Domestic sentiments. Gothic castles. Purity. If only I can reduce this pulp to pulp and spread it out into some kind of shape. Dead voices, haunting and terrible: *I want. I need. I hope. I believe.* Where'd they live? Who did their cooking? Did they expect to get pregnant every year? (See Mrs. Defoe's journal.) The awful constriction, the huge skirts. Mrs. Pepys's dress allowance ("the poor wretch" her husband called her). "How are we fall'n, fall'n by mistaken rules!" "Women live like Bats or Owls, labour like Beasts, and die like Worms." "Anyone may blame me who likes." "How good it must be to be a man when you want to travel." "John laughs at me, but one expects that in marriage." "It had all been a therapeutic lie. The mind was powerless to save her. Only a man...." "I/Revolve in my/ Sheath of impossibles—"

Scholars don't usually sit gasping and sobbing in corners of the library stacks.

But they should. They should.

In my dream the Tooth Fairy stood at the foot of my bed,

wearing an airy, blue, nylon net gown and glittering rhinestone jewelry, with a little rhinestone coronet on her head. Her magic wand was star-topped and she looked just like a Tooth Fairy should. She was going to give me three wishes.

But I woke up.

Bad weather brought Jean. A cold and blowy day with bursts of rain, a premature autumn. Her umbrella made a puddle on the landing outside my door. Tragic. Dark-eyed. Hands in raincoat pockets.

She smiled sweetly.

She said, "Ick, what weather." I had to let her in. She shed her coat, her umbrella, her packages, and her boots outside, then came into my kitchen. She was no answer to anything. She said, "Do you want to—?"

"No," I said.

"Do you want to sit in the living room?"

We sat in the living room and Jean gave me a look that said *So you're not a Lesbian any more, are you?*

I said aloud, "That's not—" and then nothing.

"Shall I tell you about Betty Botter?" she said. "You know: 'Betty Botter bought a bit of bitter butter. Said Betty Botter, This bit of bitter butter, It will make my batter bitter. So Betty Botter bought a bit of better butter and it made her batter better.'"

"What on earth—" I said.

"Blenderblunder. Betsy Batter. Batterburger. My rifle. She's in your kitchen, all wrapped up."

I said, "Who were you staying with in Boston?"

"Other Lesbians," said Jean comfortably.

Now I had done something terrible the day before that I haven't told you: I had been attracted to somebody else. I had been walking towards the library when I saw this twenty-year-old coming the other way in hip-hugger jeans and a funny little knitted top that left her bare from her ribs to her belly button. A silly, ruffled sort of blouse. That's what I saw first. Then I thought *Isn't she cold?* (It was raining.) Then I just knew there was nothing so interesting in the world as that midriff; my palms yearned for it. I wanted every little girl in the world.

That's different, that's very different. That's being a you-know-what.

She said, "'Tis with our judgments as our watches; none/ Goes just alike but each believes her own."

"You're mad," I said. Dumb with rage. Her absolutely inexplicable cheerfulness.

"I got you a present," she said, hauling a little brown-paper package from somewhere in her jeans (I don't see how she could have avoided sitting on it). Generously she held it out to me. "Go on," she said.

So I took it and untied the string (some present—brown paper and string!) and unwrapped it, holding in my hand a little white box. A dead mouse? A snakeskin? A bird's skull? These would be just Jean's style. Or, more conventionally, a flea-market ring, or the female symbol with the equals sign or the clenched fist, all done in lousy embroidery.

It was a watch sitting on a folded bit of paper. It wasn't cheap; I know the kind. I don't mean jewelry-expensive, but a good one. Perhaps twenty-five dollars. An awful lot, for her.

"You always say you lose the expensive ones," said Jean the liar, "so I got you a bad one. Here." And the bit of paper—unfolded—turned out to be an advertisement for a watch set about with diamonds, with a silly lady in false eyelashes, false hair, false everything. She was wearing a Jean Harlow slip—dress, I mean—and looking adoringly into the eyes of a handsome, shadowy man whose features you could hardly make out because he was the one giving the two-thousand dollar watch; and I suppose if you have that kind of money to buy ladies (or to buy ladies presents with), you don't need a face.

Something awful is happening. Rising. I don't think I can live through it. Also the ad is making me laugh. (I mean why not eat diamonds if you want to possess them? Only they'd come out the other end in a couple of days, wouldn't they?) Jean's watch has nice, big numbers I can read and no diamonds. I started putting her present on the white strip left on my wrist by my old watch, but something terrible was happening to the room. I've had an awful shock. Like a poor worm with a pin through it. And I wish to God Jean were somewhere else. Seeing her through what they call "scalding" tears, screaming tears, hurting dreadfully.

I wept, I wept, crying against her shoulder, nasty bilious tears, aching tears; don't ever let anyone tell you it's easy. And they didn't ease me. Is it like having convulsions? I didn't want to be touched, but I did; so she put her arms around me, saying "There, there" and "Now, now" and I put mine about her, feeling the shock of allowing it all to happen, knowing I could trust her. We held each other until I stopped crying; then I said, "I want to make love right now."

She said, "Your face is all runny," wiping it with a kleenex. Then she said, "I know, but you won't come; you'll just keep having these tremendous surges of feeling. It's too distracting."

"Huh!" I said sulkily, blowing my nose. To cheer me up, she told me about a letter some poor woman had written in a newspaper advice column, asking about how could she do away with her terrible deformity because she had this secret shame, this awful thing she couldn't let anybody know: *that she had little hairs around the aureoles of her breasts.* This, of course, is exactly what Jean has. Jean thought the letter very funny, but I turned away, groaned, wrapped my arms around my stomach—a pang of desire so keen I could barely sit up. Jean roared, which is exactly what you'd expect from a heartless, sadistic Lesbian. They all chew tobacco and cuss like truck drivers. Next thing, she'll be putting out lit cigarettes on my breasts, just like a character in a book I read by C.S. Lewis who (after all) must know. She put her arms around me and gave me a fluttery kiss, such a close one, such a loving one, such a just-light-enough one that I began to understand pornography. Do you? I said, "Help, I can't wait!" so good-natured Jean pulled the curtains to and made love to me on the living room rug. We—uh—"did things," we—uh—"endured" and we—mm—"with our"—

See?

I trembled from head to foot, I really did. I didn't lift a finger, just like all those ladies in peignoirs in vampire movies. I have never been so utterly abandoned in all my life. Or so sorry when I came. (She was wrong about that.) After the third orgasm—three, count 'em, three!—but that's nothing, for a woman—I was content to lie there and throb, admiring beautiful Jean, who now wanted the same things done to her, now that I was spryer and she more languid, another kind of pleasure. So I did, trying not to laugh at the persistent memory of that poor woman so tormented by her shameful deformity that she had to write a newpaper about it. Sex, when it's good (but how often is it that?) is like nothing on earth. So silly, so grand. So indecent, so matter-of-fact.

Much later I said, peering through the curtains, "It's stopped raining. Nasty, though."

Jean said, "Get dressed and come into the kitchen, O.K.? I want to show you Blunderbess."

She added, "You ought to learn how to shoot."

The next day I was as paranoid as ever, smiling nervously at the men in the library, trying to keep my eyes off the women. I-know-they're-all-laughing-at-me-because-even-if-they-aren't-I-deserve-it.

Sex doesn't last.

That night I had a conversation with the Tooth Fairy. She came and sat down on the end of my bed, looking very benevolent, spreading out her blue nylon net skirts, and recalling to me (even in the middle of my dream) where I had seen her before—she was somebody I saw in a live stage show when I was eight and I'd swear it was the Ice Follies because I remember her in ice skates.

THE TOOTH FAIRY: Good evening, dear child. I am here to help you.

ME: Mmmmpf! What?

THE FAIRY: Tell me what you want and I shall get it for you.

ME: Thanks but no thanks ha ha. (My standards of wit are pretty lousy in dreams.)

THE FAIRY: Shall I restore to you your lost heterosexuality, so that you may once again adore on the Late Late Show handsome actors such as Buster Crabbe, Dirk Bogarde, James Mason, and Christopher Lee?—leaving it to you to determine what common characteristics (if any) animate this rather peculiar list because, my dear, (to be perfectly frank) you have the damnedest tastes I ever saw.

ME: Not on your life.

THE FAIRY: Shall I give you the gift of sixty million dollars?

ME: You haven't got it.

THE FAIRY: Shall I give you the gift of being attracted to real men?

ME (sitting straight up in bed, in terror): No, no, no, no, no!

THE FAIRY (crossing one leg over the other, thus revealing that she was indeed wearing ice skates, great big clumpy white ones): Well, what *do* you want, for goodness sakes! Don't be difficult. Tell me your heart's desire.

There was a long, puzzled silence in my by now very symbolic bedroom. What do I want? Health? Riches? Fame? Beauty? Travel? Success? The Respect Of My Colleagues? Do I want to become a saint? (God forbid.) I've wanted all those things in my time. Like the news of the day that runs round and round the top of that building on forty-second street in New York, so little sneaky tags and proverbs ran over the ceiling, now in neon lights, now in electric light-bulbs: It is better to marry than to have a career, Somebody lovely has just passed by, Always give Daddy the biggest piece of steak, It is Woman's job to keep the stars in their courses. None of this helps, of course.

I said, "My dearest desire—"

I said, "Some time in my life—"

I said, "What I really want—"

I said, "I want to kill someone."

Then I amended it. Not a woman. Certainly not a child, not of either sex.

I said: *I want to be able to kill a man.*

I said to Jean, "Why is wanting to be able to kill a man so bizarre? *Men* kill men. Watch TV. Men kill *women* on TV."

"Monopolistic practices," said Jean.

We were in her back yard, standing in the premature autumn leaves, shooting at tin cans. I hoped the neighborhood cats would have sense enough to be warned off by the noise, unlike the two-legged kind of cat, who is so often attracted by sounds like that. No rabbits, either. Just tin cans. I once ran over a dog with my car—not meaning to, of course—I was driving into the sunset and hardly saw him until he was right in front of me. I slowed down to twenty and he went right between the wheels; I felt him bumping against the floorboards (and heard him yelping) but he limped away fast, so perhaps he wasn't killed. It was an awful, hateful thing, worse in some ways than hurting a human being because animals can have no intentions toward you. Not real ones.

Bam! Jean is patiently trying to correct a tendency she has to pull to one side. Inherited from archery practice, probably. A strange, respectably dressed Professorial type appeared in the gap in the front hedge only half an hour ago, saying, amused—as if it were any of his business!—"What are you girls doing?" (As I told you, I'm thirty-eight.)

Jean had swung the gun round, quite coldly. And pulled back the safety catch. "Get out!" He turned pale and backed away, vanished behind the hedge. As if it were his business, you know, as if everything women did was naturally his business.

Against the wire fence at the back of the yard one early maple sapling flames up—pure scarlet. Such useless rage. I used to think I felt like a failure because I was neurotic, because I was over-sensitive, because I'd had a bad childhood (who hasn't), because I lacked that seventh outermost layer of skin that everyone is supposed to have; I said it was the price I paid for being an intellectual. I cried over it. I used to hate you so; I used to dream of killing you over and over again. I used to wonder, with an awe beyond all jealousy, what it was you had that protected you so, that made Rose fall in love with you (over and over again!), what peace, what blessing, what infinite favor in the eyes of God.

Bam!

Jean is, I suspect, holding it.

Bam!

(Any sensible rabbit would have fled long ago. The tin can jerks mechanically.)

"I'm pulling to the left," Jean says.

"Oh Jean, *symbols!*"

There's no sillier activity, practically speaking (or so it seems to me) than shooting tin cans in one's own back yard. Tin cans aren't alive. I don't want to get tin cans out of my way. Yet if men take to it like ducks to water (as a sign of the position in life to which it has pleased God to call them) I think I will practice anyway. I have been shooting all afternoon; my back hurts, my elbows hurt, my skirt's damp and stained from the leaves. Even long, lovely Indian skirts won't do for this sort of activity; first you "break" it, then you eject the used cartridge, then you put it back together again (like a stapler, see?), then you flop down on your stomach, then you push off the what-chamacallit (safety catch), then you brace it against your shoulder, which is going to hurt like blooming blazes before the day is over.

The Tooth Fairy floats down out of the crowded gray heaven, flops on a pile of leaves, and remains there, so shocked as to be nearly invisible. She watches us, bereft of words.

"Jean," I said, "what d'you do with a man you've shot?"

"Leave him alone, dear; he's not much good dead. Nobody is."

"Would you bring him back to life?"

"Dunno. Maybe. Maybe not. I'd probably have to shoot him again."

Bam!

Jean says angrily, "Oh damn, this blasted Bettybop's doing the Charleston. I'm tired." She sits up. "Will you do my shoulders?" So I kneel over her, trying to make like a backrub the best I can, and composing in my mind the following letter to my ex-friend Rose (see p. 1 paragraph 1) which I will entrust to the Tooth Fairy to deliver when it is finished:

"Dear Rose,

How are you? Do you still commit psychic incest with persons bigger, brighter, stronger, richer, more successful, and in every way better than yourself? Do you look for hours at lipsticks in store windows? Are you beautiful?

"My friend and I have just finished viciously murdering 4 rabbits, 3 tree stumps, 8 pieces of paper, and 6 unwary cats with a rifle called Bloodyborebingle. It is a bloody bore (bingle). It sings magically when we take it out of its wrappings and howls every time we shoot it. It wants blood. It wants us to shoot MEN and hang their stuffed intestines on our wall. My friend and I spit on the ground and cuss a lot. We have cut our hair. We flex our muscles in public and wear leather jackets. Are we revolting? You bet!

"The weather here is fine. Winter is coming. Soon it will be too dark to shoot most of the time, so I am concentrating on reading, though frankly there isn't much I can stand, so I am sticking to the diary of Mrs. Daniel Defoe. Mrs. Daniel Defoe is not to be confused with Mr. Daniel Defoe; he has the names and is the man, so don't get them mixed up. I am also writing my own history, which is about how an unstable (tho' pretty) young girl beset by Indefinable Rapture can be corrupted (due to the lack of proper guidance) into a hopeless, happy, neurotic feminist militant invert. You may not know what "invert" means so you had better look it up. It is actually a word used to describe sugar and is synonymous with levulose or dextrose, I forgot which. My story is a warning to all parents, all children, and all psychiatrists.

"Do you still fear to dress in velvet because it is sensuous?

"Do you still think Shakespeare is all about fathers and daughters?

"Do you still think your breasts are ugly?

"I have beautiful breasts but you would not like them, so don't visit. The weather here's too bracing.

Surrealistically yours,
Esther.

"P.S. We are on strike against God."

TOOTH FAIRY: I refuse to deliver that ghastly, obscene communication.

ME (coarsely): Buzz off! You were undoubtedly demoted from Fairy Godmother because of sheer incompetence.

TOOTH FAIRY (spitting on her ice skate blades): Never! Never!

ME: Off! Or I will have you sent back to painting goldenrods.

Jean said, "What are you whispering about?"

"I'm creating," I said.

"Would you stop creating and put your rugose tentacle here, eh?" said Jean, indicating her shoulder under her collar. "It hurts." She's begun to purr.

I said, "Jean, I am willing to come out, but not in the back yard under the eyes of the neighbors."

"Then let's go in," she said.

The amazing peacefulness, the astonishing lack of anger, the sweetness and balm of being at last on the right side of power.

You'll meet us. I'll tell you that the invisible stars I talked about earlier are called Black Holes—but that's too-heavy symbolism; we think I'll keep that to ourselves.

You're Stevie. I'll write you. We're still old friends, at least for a while. Are your friends like you? Are your lovers like you? I just don't know. (I must write Sally and Louise, too, but at greater length.)

You can't recognize us in a crowd. Don't try.

You think Jean and I will go away like ladies and live in the country with Stupid Philpotts and the cats. We won't.

You think we're not middle-aged. You think we're not old.

You even think we're not married. (We might be, even to you.)

Worst of all, you think we're still furiously angry at you, that we need you, that we hate you, that we scrabble desperately at your sleeve, crying "Let me go! Let me go!" We've seen you smirk a little over this, sometimes in public and sometimes secretly in the mirror when you thought no one was looking. You're right, because there is an Esther who still hates and needs you but she never liked you (that was the giveaway) and every day she fades a little more. She cared horribly when you said guns were penises so she couldn't have one, that pens were penises so she couldn't have one, that checkbooks were penises so she couldn't have one, that minds were penises so she couldn't have one. (It astonishes all of us, this monopoly on symbols.)

When I smile flatteringly at you, we're a liar.

When we hate and need you, I'm dangerous.

When they become indifferent, run for your life.

At this point some hapless liberal sees the end-papers approaching and has started looking frantically for the Reconciliation Scene. It (the liberal) is either cursing itself for having got entrapped in what started as a perfectly harmless story of love, poignancy, tragedy, self-hatred, and death, or—rather smugly—is disapproving of me for not possessing Shakespeare's magnificent gift of reconciliation which (if you translate it) means that at this point I must (1) meet a wonderful, ideal man and fall in love with him, or (2) kill myself.

You write it.

The way to do it is this: (1) give up your job, (2) become impotent, (3) go on Welfare, (4) crawl on your hands and knees both to the Welfare people and your sex partners, and (5) just for the hell of it, turn Black.

Now you can write a *perfectly beautiful* reconciliation scene.

You are the liberal who might concede (if pushed into a corner and yelled at by twenty angry radicals) that morality does indeed begin at the mouth of a gun (though you'd add quickly, "It doesn't end there") but do you realize what does end at the mouth of a gun? Fear. Frustration. Self-hate. Everything romantic. (This depends, of course, on being at the proper end of the gun.)

You are the teenage male student who comes to us saying O teachur teachur why teachest not thou Conan the Conqueror, Brak the Barbarian, and Douglas the Dilettante, they are mightye of thewe and arme, O teachur, teach yon mighty heroes of olde, pray pray. To which we answer, Sirrah student thou jestest tee hee ho ho what interest hath a Woman of Reason in yon crappe? To which thou sayest, That is not crappe, O blind teachur, but Great Art and Universale; it is all about Myghty Male Feats and Being an Hero, appealing alike to yonge and old, hye and lowe, Blakke and Whyt. To which we reply Buzz off, thou Twerp, thou hast of sexism and acne a galloping case feh feh.

You—oh, what a *nuisance* you are!—will some day soon see us on TV asked at a demonstration, or someone like me until she turns round (you can't pick them out of a crowd)—

Interviewer: Who are you?

We (smiling): Oh, somebody. A woman.

Interviewer (he's getting insistent): But what's your name?

And we'll say very lightly and quickly: My name is Legion.

My father once taught me to shoot the same way he taught me to play chess—badly, so he could beat me. He showed me Fool's Mate (so I could avoid it, he said) and then insisted that I play before I'd even memorized what the pieces were supposed to do, before I felt comfortable with them. He then gave me Fool's Mate twice.

I'm a quick learner. We all are. We never played again. Just as we never shot again. Just as we never challenged him again.

Until now.

Jean went to New Zealand. She got her degree, got a job there, and left.

I went to my first Lesbian bar.

It's a gloomy place converted from an old garage and has been bombed twice, not by bigots but by the Mafia, who run the other gay bar in town. They did it late at night when there was nobody in it, which was thoughtful of them, sort of.

I met a big, fat, low-income woman with a ducktail haircut.

I *really do* object to the low income and so does she.

I was introduced to her by a nervous, wide-eyed, twenty-year-old who'd never finished high school and who told me a long, complicated story (cracking gum) about an English teacher who accused her of plagiarism when she was writing an essay about religion, which she felt very keenly because at the time she'd been planning to become a nun. When she found out what I did for a living ("An English teacher!" she said in dismay) she was very kind anyway; she insisted on playing a game of TV ping pong with me and then took me around and introduced me gravely to everyone in the bar. I ended up sitting next to the big, fat, &c., with whom I cried a little, about Jean's leaving, but then I perked up when she asked me to dance. I felt like an awful fool, dancing, because I hadn't done it since I was twelve in summer camp (and then we only learned to rhumba, for some peculiar reason) but she felt so good. So lovely and blessed, as upholstered people do. Which surprised me. So we wandered around the floor for a bit and then went to my place because a converted garage with dim lights is pretty depressing (she said it first) and I cried some more.

She showed me her great lavender hat (a cap with a visor) and told me what it's like to drive a taxi. I cheered up.

We made love, nervously.

You know, I am an awful snob. Or I have been an awful snob, but if it's possible to be miserable once and then not, one doesn't have to stay a snob, either.

It was all you, you, you (poor you!), secret guerilla warfare and I won't let you play on my affections; I'm allowed to joke about it but only on my back, this wicked, deadly, ghastly, losing, murderous folly you so genially, so cheerfully, and so jokingly insist on.

But there's another you. Are you out there? Can you hear me? We're going to meet a dozen times a day. You'll be in my c.r. group and you'll say you can't stand Lesbians, Lesbians are terrible, they're horrible, and I'll say (in a small voice, trying not to crawl under the sofa), "But I'm a Lesbian," and you'll say, "Oh," so much in an "Oh," so many worlds in an "Oh."

We'll joke across a store-counter, eyes meeting, across a mimeo machine, talk haltingly in a laundromat, saying, "Yes, I didn't think it would go up to eighty today," or "Yes, it's awful to drive in snow," meaning, "Yes, I know." Women who'd hate me if you knew; you don't want to hear about libbers and you certainly don't want to hear about the other thing, either, but still there's that amazing bond, following each other around the office tentatively, primitive Democracy, bits of words exchanged in the margins of Serious, Important, Public Life, little sympathies, women with silly gestures, women with self-deprecating laughs, women with too many smiles, women who wear white gloves, and under it all the most amazing toughness.

Once a week I get an airmail letter with an efflorescent

stamp, a koala bear or a rhododendron, New Zealand, of all places.

Students who follow me with slitted eyes, with their private journals, with hankerchiefs balled in their fists, because they must talk all about Charlotte Brontë or die.

You're alone. You've had a bad time. You'd rather not talk to anyone, it's much safer, and yet somehow—imprudently— you do, every chance you get. You say the most amazing things to virtual strangers. You know whom you can trust.

You say nasty things about women and laugh, get tense and furious in the presence of women intellectuals, career women, man-haters, unChristian harpies.

You give me cookies and tea anyway because I look like a nice lady and you don't know it but you're right; I am a nice lady.

You have wonderful memories: a hat with a striped ribbon at age eight, waving at a troop train in World War One, being carried in a parade holding a sign that said Votes for Women, having to wear knickers and being forbidden to play with the neighbor cat, a baleful Persian tom with green eyes, whom you loved.

You breed cats. You ride. You fix cars. You can't stand my mother. Sometimes you are my mother. You write awful stories in my classes about women who work in factories (you know less than nothing about them) and whose husbands beat them and who are simple and elemental and who forgive everyone, and in the middle of these stale and dreadful fictions you put your own frightening, beautiful, terrible, vivid dreams.

You're Rose.

You go quietly mad in little backwaters, worry about your kids, tell everybody what's wrong with today's children, hate your mother, mutter aloud in department stores, say awful things in public to my friend's crippled daughter, drag yourself out at thirteen (one leg in a brace) to learn to ride horses. You're the radical so ready to destroy yourself that you intimidate me. You write letters to local papers in which you condemn all the working women in the world, all the Black people in the world, all the pot-smoking students, and all the radicals who would defile the promise of America, and you sign them, "A Christian American Anti-hippie Mother."

What can I say to you? You're more various than that. How can I love you properly? How can I praise you properly? How can I make love to you properly? How can I tell you never to kill for pleasure, never to kill for sport, never to kill for cruelty, but above all, don't play fair, because when they invite you in, remember: we aren't playing.

You teach introductory University biology, cry "Pull yourself togethah!" to your less-than-Spartan friends, and charge up mountains at forty-three, working like ten women, carrying a baby while you teach five classes, running a farm, dyeing your stiff British hair, and intimidating everyone with that upper-class British voice in which you tell us all—so thrillingly—to be Strong.

You live on unemployment, keeping gas money in a cut-off milk carton in the front of your car, fixing four or five cars for a hobby, getting full of grease most of the time, wearing your hair curled above your square jaw like Anna Magnani, whom you say you look like (and you do), and spending brow-knotted hours braiding macramé plant holders for geraniums.

You smile a lot and retreat a lot and discover strange things about mesons, very quiet, very shy, always losing things out of the pocket of your lab coat, deferential to your husband, deferential to everybody, always looking as if you had just said, "What?"

You're my Polish grandmother, bad-tempered and selfish, an immigrant at seventeen to a country that was not paved with gold after all, throwing dishware at your two daughters in a rage until they hid out of range on the porch roof, yet calmly taking a hot iron away from a crazy countrywoman, saying, "Sophie, dolling, you don't mean it. Give me the iron."

You're my friend Carolellen, who dressed as a Russian Maiden in summer camp when we had the costume party, fascinated by lipsticks and blue-tinted stockings at twelve, short-tempered, crying once because you thought somebody was letting a pet salamander die (you were so theatrical about that!), not wanting to hear about sexual intercourse from the camp counselor because you knew married people just felt each other up, and falling in love with your cousin who, to my mind, resembled a long, lanky, newt, but insisting that sex had nothing to do with it; it was his beautiful soul.

You write me letters about my books, saying, "Do you know what it's like to find yourself in literature only as a bad metaphor?" and you sign them "Empress of the Universe" and "A Reader" and "A Struggling Poet" and "A Married Woman." You say, "I liked your book and am sending it to my daughter, who is a telephone lineman in Florida."

Hello. Hello, out there. Have you met Jean in New Zealand? Did you meet somebody you thought might be Jean? That's enough. Did you think you had no allies? What I want to say is, there are all of us; what I want to say is, we're all in it together; what I want to say is, it's not just me, though I'm waving, too; I've hung my red petticoat out on a stick and I'm signalling like mad, I'm trying to be seen, too. But there are more of us.

You once sent me a poem. I have an awful feeling you may send me thousands of poems. I can't read them. I'll have to put them in my waterbed. (I haven't got a waterbed.) I'll have to feed them to my camel. (I haven't got a camel.) It's too many poems for one woman to read, but we should all trade poems, we should all talk like mad and whoop and dance like mad, traveling in caravans and on camel-back (great, gorgeous, sneery eyes, haven't they?) and elephant-howdah and submarine and hot-air balloon and canoes and unicycles and just plain shanks' mare towards that Great Goddess-Thanksgiving Dinner in the sky; Jean can rough-house with Stupid Philpotts and tie his hair back with a red ribbon and then roll up her sleeves and make her batter better.

We must all get some better butter; that will make our batter better.

The shirtwaist workers who went on strike started just by going on strike, but then they discovered things; they discovered picketing and unity and museums and *Les Miserables* and Marx and journalism and racism* and parks and love and work and how to cook and each other. I like to think they had

*Well, they *began* to. Some of them. Sort of.

fights about whether trade unionism meant feminism and feminism meant Lesbianism and Lesbianism meant trade unionism and so forth.

So hello. It's beginning. I don't care who you sleep with, I really don't, you know, as long as you love me. As long as I can love all of you. Honk if you love us. Float a ribbon, a child's balloon, a philodendron, your own hair, out the car window. Let's be for us. For goodness' sakes, let's not be against us. Somebody (female?) scrawled on a wall at the Sorbonne the most sensible comment of the twentieth century and it must have been a woman; I will bet a postage stamp (with a koala on it) that it was a woman.* She looked around her and she knitted her brow** and then she wrote what I think we should all follow, not to excess, of course,*** but to excess, because the Road to Excess leads absolutely everywhere, William Blake, q.v. (who was sort of one of us but not nearly enough, not to excess, not to wisdom).****

She wrote:
*Let's be reasonable. Let's demand the impossible.*****

*I do not have in my possession at the moment a postage stamp with a koala bear on it. I do have, however, a postage stamp with a picture of the New Zealand rhododendron on it (stylized). I'll bet that one.

**Actually she may not have done this; she may simply have written it. You don't have to make a face, though it helps.

***Heavens, no.

****He proposed to his wife, one hot summer's day, that they take off their flesh and sit in the garden in their bones. She did better. She knew better. She sat in the garden in her naked soul.

*****Right!

******A foot note without a referent.

*******Another.

********And another. By far the best kind.

*********Yet another.

**********A perfectly blank footnote.

***********This one is special. It's for Jean.

************This one is *very* special. It ends the book. It is for you.

JOANNA RUSS's other novels are *Picnic on Paradise* (Ace, 1969), *And Chaos Died* (Ace, 1970), *The Female Man* (Bantam, 1975) *Alyx* (G. K. Hall, 1976), *We Who Are About To* (Dell, 1977), *The Two of Them* (Putnam, 1978), and *Kittatinny: a Tale of Magic* (Daughters Publishing Co., Inc., 1978).

She has two collections of essays: *How to Suppress Women's Writing Without Really Trying* (University of Texas Press, 1984) and *Magic Mommas, Trembling Sisters, Puritans and Perverts* (The Crossing Press, 1985). A work of fiction, *Extra (Ordinary) People*, was published by St. Martin's Press in 1984. Her reviews have appeared in *The Magazine of Fantasy and Science Fiction*, *Frontiers: a Journal of Women Studies*, and *The Washington Post*. She currently teaches writing at the University of Washington in Seattle.